STEALING THE MARSHAL'S HEART

EMMA JAY

PROLOGUE

New Mexico Territory, 1875

SHOUTING WOKE ELEVEN-YEAR-OLD ABIGAIL VINCENT. She lifted her head and looked across the small room at her little brother Abe, who slept on, one hand above his head on the pillow, his lips parted on easy breaths, his raven-black hair blending with the shadows.

Her own shoulders tight, she slipped from bed to investigate. She squeezed her eyes shut as she opened the door, praying it didn't creak and give her away. But no, with all the noise coming from the kitchen, no one could possibly hear it. She padded barefoot down the hall to peer into the kitchen. Her mother stood, bracing her arms on the end of the table where six men sat, all of them talking at the same time so that Abigail couldn't make out the words.

Abigail dropped to her knees by the door, out of the line of sight and watched impatience play across her mother's beautiful face. Sweetheart Belle was the name the papers had given her, a soft name for a hard woman, a woman who ran a crew of outlaws that robbed banks and trains all across the West. The men surrounding Belle now, including Abe's father, Joseph Two Rivers Running, who leaned against the sink with his arms folded over his massive chest, were only part of her crew. And it sounded as though they were planning a train robbery.

Abigail sat and wrapped her arms around her legs, pulling them tight to her chest. From the way her mother was dressed, in dungarees and layered shirts, Abigail knew they were riding out tonight. Abigail shuddered when she glanced toward the closed door behind which Joseph's mother slept. She loathed staying alone with the old woman, who hated her mother and, by extension, Abigail, but doted on little Abe. She wondered how long her mother would be gone this time.

Belle slapped a hand on the table and got the attention of the men. Abigail scanned the faces that she could see, and not for the first time she wondered if one of those men was her father. More than one of them had shared her mother's bed, sometimes more than one at the same time. They still did, on occasion, when Joseph was away. But when she'd asked her mother about her father, Belle had only laughed and dismissed the question.

Abigail focused on her mother's words, on the route they planned to take, on which hill they'd crest to approach the train, which car they were aiming for, what the haul would be. Abigail said a little prayer, first that the heist would go well. Her mother and Joseph would stomp around like angry bears for weeks if anything went wrong.

And she said a little prayer for the safety of the people on the train. Abigail knew her mother's determination to get what she wanted, knew she wouldn't hesitate to stop anyone in her way.

It never occurred to her to say a prayer for the safety of her mother.

* * *

ABIGAIL ESCAPED to the creek two days later. Her mother and the others hadn't returned, not unusual. Many times they'd be gone for weeks, taking the long way around so the law couldn't follow them back here to the New Mexico ranch. This was the first home she'd had in her short life, having spent most of the time camping or moving from one place to another. She didn't want to have to move again.

But today she needed to get away from Joseph's mother, Little Snow. Abigail had said she was going to fetch water, anything to get away from the sour woman, but instead she stood in the water to her ankles and let the fish nibble her toes. The water was almost too cold already, but she liked the feel of it rushing over her skin.

She saw the dust from the horses from a distance, and her heart leapt. Was her mother back so soon? She slipped on a rock in her haste to get out of the creek, and went down on one knee, hard enough to see stars. But she pushed past the pain and scrambled onto the bank, ignoring her wet skirts, the dirt that clung to her feet as she bolted up the rise toward the house.

As she grew closer, though, her elation faded. Not enough riders. Not enough. Urgency propelled her onward. Perhaps the crew had split up. Perhaps some of them were still in a nearby town, spending their spoils.

But none of the men sitting on the horses in the yard were familiar. All of them turned to her when she stopped short, her lungs burning, her head swimming. The flash of sunlight through a cloud glinted off of a silver star on one of the men's coat.

The law. If she'd had any strength in her legs, she would run the other direction, back to the creek, far away. Instead she just stood there as the big man turned his horse toward her.

From birth, she'd been trained to fear the law, but something in this man's lined, weathered face seemed kind, a trait at odds with the gun at his belt and the rifle slung across the back of his saddle. She took a step back, and a second man pulled his horse around, probably ready to run her down if she fled. She chanced a glance at his face, and saw his expression wasn't threatening either. He was younger than the lawman, dark-haired, with the most beautiful blue eyes she'd ever seen, blue eyes that watched her with sympathy.

She couldn't say how she knew, but she did, even before the lawman spoke.

"Are you Sweetheart Belle's daughter?"

She forced herself to nod, though her neck was stiff with dread. She didn't want to hear the words and lifted her hands to her ears, as if that would stop the truth.

"Your mother is dead."

CHAPTER 1

$\mathcal{N}$*ine years later*

ABIGAIL HUNG the laundry on the line and cursed the wind that chilled her chapped hands. No sense wearing gloves that would only get wet, and the laundry had to be done. She'd been in the George P. Williamson Home for Wayward Girls for four years now, two as a resident and two as a servant, since she had no other place to go.

For two years after her mother died, she'd lived with Joseph Two Rivers Running, Little Snow and Abe. She'd done her best to mother Abe, though Little Snow wrested him away from her every chance she got. Joseph himself had spent the first year after Belle's death drowning his sorrows in a bottle. While he'd been a violent man in his career, and occasionally violent with Belle when he got in a jealous rage, he wasn't a violent drunk and had simply ignored Abigail and Abe.

They'd moved immediately after Belle's death. Joseph had come in the night for them and taken them all away. Abigail was fairly certain he would have left her behind if he thought he could get away with it. She was nothing to him. They'd moved to a farm in the southern part of the territory, where they'd kept to themselves.

Some of Joseph's friends visited, and Joseph would go off for a few days, which helped her breathe easier. One of his friends, Daniel Holland, brought his younger brother Nate. Nate was a handsome boy, with dark blonde curls that always flipped up under the brim of his hat and a wicked smile that made her awakening body tingle. She let him catch her in the barn, let him nudge her against a wall, let him teach her how to kiss. He wanted more, but she captured his hands when they would slide down over her breasts, though she suspected his touch would feel good.

Her newly aware body sensed danger when Joseph looked at her. Not when he was drunk, but when he was sober, she saw a look in his eyes that scared her enough to block the door to her room every night.

That didn't stop him from cornering her in the kitchen one morning when she was cleaning up from breakfast.

"You look so much like her," he said.

For a moment, she didn't know he was talking to her. He never addressed her directly. But then he turned her toward him and cupped his hand over her cheek. When he lowered his head, she panicked and shoved at his chest with all her might, but he was too big, too strong. And sober.

A smile curved his lips. "She liked to play rough, too."

Fear bubbled in her throat when she realized his intention. What had seemed like fun with Nate was suddenly terrifying. She struggled in his arms, letting out a small shriek of alarm.

"So like her," he said, and covered her mouth with his.

She'd pressed her lips tightly shut against his invading tongue, which only made him pull her closer against him. On a few occasions, he and her mother had been indiscreet, and she'd seen them couple, knew exactly what he was pressing against her.

"You were willing for that boy in the barn. Let a man show you."

Terror iced her veins, and she twisted violently, surprising him into releasing her. She whirled to flee, and came face to face with his mother.

The next few weeks were miserable as she tried to make herself invisible. And when Nate and Daniel returned, she left the farm with them. She'd been fourteen years old.

Which was how she'd ended up here. Mrs. McBride had hired her as a maid when she'd become too old to remain a resident. The strict rules still chafed her spirit—she'd spent the first thirteen years of her life running wild, with no rules—but at least she was safe.

"Miss Vincent! You have a visitor."

Abigail pivoted to face the house mother, clutching the wet sheet against her. Mrs. McBride stood on the wooden steps, arms folded beneath her ample breasts. Abigail could sense her displeasure across the yard, but that was secondary to the alarm that rose in Abigail's chest. No one had been to see her since she'd come here. She'd watched visitors come for some of the other girls, but no one had ever come to see her. She had no one. No one but...

"Abe!" She dropped the wet sheet into the dirt and hurried forward, her feet tangling in the linens a moment before she gained her balance and ran toward the house. She slowed only as she passed Mrs. McBride, dipping her head in apology as she passed her.

Mrs. McBride huffed and turned to follow, but Abigail hit her stride on the hardwood floor, skidding to a stop when she reached the parlor.

The man who unfolded himself from the settee, holding his hat in front of him, wasn't Abe. This man was a stranger, but familiar somehow with his chiseled features, dark hair to his broad shoulders and the bluest eyes she had ever seen.

She took a step back to encounter Mrs. McBride, who had caught up with her.

"Miss Vincent, this is Marshal Marcus Grey."

Belatedly she saw the star on his jacket and took another step back. The last time she'd seen him, he'd told her that her mother was dead. The tightness of his lips told her he didn't have good news for her now, either.

Her first instinct was to dash out the front door and keep running. *Abe.* It had to be about Abe. He was the only thing she had left.

"Miss Vincent, I'm sorry. I'm here about your brother."

Even though she knew it was coming, her knees went weak and she staggered. The marshal caught her arms, as if he'd been expecting it. His hands were strong, long-fingered, and he guided her to the settee. She realized, as she lowered to it, that she'd been here four years and never sat in this room.

"He's dead?"

"No. No, ma'am." He crouched in front of her. "He's not dead. But his father has gotten him involved with a bad bunch. He's a fugitive right now, and I thought maybe he'd come here."

Something loosened in her chest. "Not dead?"

"No, but he's on a path that will lead to the grave. Do you have any idea where he might be?"

"I haven't seen him in six years." She couldn't reconcile the picture of the boy she'd left behind with the person the marshal was speaking about. But the boy she'd known would want to please his father. She understood that. She also believed that Joseph Two Rivers Running would ask this of his son. She looked into the sympathetic blue eyes. "He's only fifteen."

"Yes, I know."

"What will happen when you catch him?"

The marshal straightened and backed away to sit in another

chair that looked too frail to hold his weight. "Well, at the moment, he's accused of armed robbery, but we don't believe he's killed anyone. If I can get to him soon, before a posse does, I can keep him alive."

She twisted her hands in her skirts. "I never should have left him behind." The decision had torn her in two, but she'd thought he'd be fine, there with his grandmother who adored him and his own father. She hadn't taken into account that Joseph would pull him into the outlaw life. In the two years after her mother's death, Joseph had stayed on the straight and narrow. She'd thought he'd left his outlaw ways behind after losing the love of his life.

The marshal rose, turning his hat in front of him. "All right, then, I thank you. But if he comes, if you see him, you tell him he needs to turn himself in, or it will go bad for him."

He nodded at her, and at Mrs. McBride, who still stood in the doorway, her disapproval evident in the crease between her eyebrows. He walked out the front door and Abigail remained on the couch, her legs still shaky, her mind whirling.

"You'd best get up and finish that laundry," Mrs. McBride said with a cluck of her tongue.

Abigail gripped the arm of the settee for a moment before launching to her feet. She headed outside—but not out back to the laundry. She charged through the front door in time to see the marshal mounting his horse.

"I want to come with you."

He angled his hat back on his head. "No, ma'am. You can't do that."

"If you find him, he might try to do something stupid, like try to shoot you, and then where would he be? I can talk to him."

"Ma'am, it's hard riding, sleeping out in the cold, and just the two of us, without a chaperone. I don't have the time or the funds to take care of your reputation."

"Marshal, I'm Sweetheart Belle's daughter. I have no reputation. Let me come with you."

He shook his head. "No, ma'am. I'll keep you apprised." He touched the brim of his hat and wheeled his horse away.

* * *

MARCUS SHED his shirt and bent over the basin. The water was a little colder than he'd like, but he splashed it on his face anyway, feeling his nipples tighten with the shock, his balls draw up. He hadn't stayed in a hotel in weeks, and would like a proper bath, but now he was too tired. He grabbed the nearby towel and rubbed it over his face just as the knock came at the door.

Frowning, he reached without stepping and opened the door to see a young man standing there, wearing baggy denims, two shirts, and a bandana around his neck, his hat tipped down. He frowned—why was he wearing a hat inside? But then the young man lifted his head and Marcus took a step back. He knew those amber eyes.

"Miss Vincent, what are you doing here? And in those clothes?" Where had she gotten them at a home for girls? And how had she gotten to town?

She slipped into his room and closed the door before she removed her hat and glared at him. Damn, she was pretty, prettier even than her mother had been, with just a hint of the same wildness.

"I have to find my brother."

"That's my job."

"I can't stay here knowing he's in trouble. And now I've run away from the home, and Mrs. McBride will never accept me back." She lifted her chin. "I need to go with you."

He shook his head and reached for his shirt, dragging it over his head. "It's not proper. Not proper for you to be here, either. Did you walk to town?"

Color flooded her cheeks. "I rode."

"You stole a horse?"

"Borrowed. I have money I saved from working at the home. I can buy a horse of my own, and leave the home's horse here in Fortune. If we send word, Mrs. McBride can have someone pick it up. The livery sells horses, don't they?"

"Not one that can keep up the pace I'm setting. And what are you thinking, that you'll just stay here tonight?" He waved his hand toward the bed.

This time she took a step back. "I can sleep in the stable."

He scowled at his bed, the one he'd looked forward to sleeping in. He should let her. He hadn't invited her—had told her he didn't want her to come, in fact. But if he sent her into the barn to freeze, he'd never be able to sleep.

He glanced at the window—too late to take her back tonight. So he grabbed up his belongings, shoving them back into his pack and heaved it onto his shoulder. "In the morning, you're going back."

She flinched at his tone, then took a step forward and placed her hand on his chest. "I can stay in here with you."

He looked from her work-roughened hand against his white shirt to the amber eyes that betrayed her nerves. His scowl deepened even as his cock jumped at her touch. She'd grown up with outlaws—maybe she'd never met an honorable man before. That he was her first annoyed him more than he cared to admit. He brushed past her and headed to the stable.

* * *

SHE WAS WAITING for him in the dining room of the hotel when he came in the next morning. The hat was back on her head, but he wondered who she thought she was fooling. Her face was smooth, her eyes unmistakably feminine. She sat at a table in the back, a plate of biscuits in front of her. He wondered if, like the room, he was paying for her breakfast. He crossed to her, removing his hat and hanging it on the hook by the wall.

Thank God there weren't more customers, though he couldn't be sure if it was the hour, the town, or the food. He sat in the high-backed wooden chair across from her and hoped it wasn't the food, though the pieces she'd nibbled on but left on her plate didn't bode well.

The proprietor, a paunchy man wearing a vest and sideburns practically to his chin dropped a plate with a full meal in front of him—biscuits, gravy, eggs and sausage.

"She says she's with you," the man said in a gravelly voice. "Said she's your prisoner."

Marcus leveled a look at her. "Is that so."

"Damnedest thing I ever saw, a prisoner waiting for the marshal to wake up." His face darkened when he looked at Abigail again. "We run a respectable place. You need to dress like a lady."

"My fault," Marcus heard himself saying when Abigail blanched. "We have a long day in front of us, and I told her to dress to ride. Can't have a woman ride side-saddle all the way to Texas."

The proprietor frowned. "Seems to me you'd get a stage. Or a buggy."

"Not if we want to get there before the new year. We'll settle up when we're done here."

The man gave Abigail one last disgusted look and turned away at Marcus's dismissal.

"So you'll take me with you?"

He heard the hope in her voice as he sipped his coffee. At least the beverage was flavorful, which made him hopeful for breakfast. If he hadn't been able to sleep in a real bed last night, at least he wanted a good hot meal.

"Taking you back to the home."

She gripped her fork so hard, he thought she might stab him. "I can't. Mrs. McBride will never take me back."

He'd thought of that last night as he'd struggled to fall asleep in the hay in the stable, huddled inside his coat and his bedroll. "I'll talk to her, tell her how sorry you are. She'll take you back."

"Then I won't go back."

"And what are you going to do? Stay here in town by yourself?"

"I thought about it after you left. I may not know where Joseph stays now, but I do know some of the places he stayed in the past."

He narrowed his eyes. "How?"

"We didn't always have a house when I was growing up, not until the last year or so, when we lived in that place where you came to tell us about her. On occasion, my mother would stash us with friends when she'd go on her...journeys."

"Journeys. That's an interesting way to put it."

She folded her arms on the table. "I can help you find these places."

"You were just a child. And who's to say the 'friends' still live there? You moved around enough."

"I have to do something. The next time I see you, you're not coming to tell me my brother is dead, too. He's all I have left."

He felt himself softening, and shored his will up. "You said yourself he hasn't come to see you in six years. I'm thinking the connection isn't as strong as you'd like to think."

"He was just a boy, raised by a thoughtless man and an evil woman."

He lifted his eyebrows. "Your mother?"

She scowled. "His grandmother. If you don't take me with you, I'm going to go on my own to look for him."

"And you'd last about a day. Let me take you back to the home now, and save you the trouble."

She pushed to her feet. "I'm sorry you don't see the benefit of having me along, Marshal."

He was aware of the other patrons turning to look, and wanted to bury his head in his hands. He thanked his lucky stars he didn't, because then he wouldn't have been able to move as quickly as 'he did when she raised her fork and brought it down on the back of his hand.

CHAPTER 2

Two hours later, they were on their way. Again he realized he should have left her behind. He underestimated her desperation, and now cradled his injured hand against his chest. He should have left her to the sheriff and ridden off without her. Instead, he'd bought a damn horse and put her on it, and now they rode along the trail by the railroad, through the high desert, a brisk north wind keeping them company.

She managed to keep up with him, riding at a canter, not complaining, though he could tell by the tight line of her mouth that she wasn't comfortable. He had already slowed his usual pace, and the concession made him antsy.

"Is this the first time Joseph took Abe with him on a job?" she asked, her voice tight against the chill in the air.

He glanced over. "No."

"So something happened this time. Something bad?"

"A couple men were shot. Witnesses say Abe was one of the shooters."

She flinched. "Abe was a terrible shot when I knew him."

"He got better."

She shivered, and he looked toward the setting sun. Damn, he hated winter and its short days. They were going to have to find a place to camp, and soon. He didn't know this area too well, and didn't know where a good spot would be, so he needed to use the remaining light to search.

He also didn't know how hard a night Abigail was used to spending. "Ever slept outside?"

"All the time when I was young. We didn't have a house until I was almost ten."

"Really. I didn't know that. So your mother took you around with her? Place to place?"

"She would leave us, sometimes, at one of the camps, or with some friends. But yes, we wandered for a long time before she found a house."

He shifted in the saddle to look at her. "Was Joseph in her life all that time? I mean, he's not your father, is he?"

"No, not my father. My mother never told me who my father was."

"But Joseph? He was around during this time? He would know some of these places?"

She straightened. "That's what I'm hoping."

He blew out a breath and drew up his horse at the top of the rise. Below he saw a sheltered outcropping and nudged his horse down the hill toward it.

Abigail sat on her horse for a moment when they reached the campsite, which offered shelter that would let them build a fire out of the wind. He squinted up at her in the growing shadows.

"You going to get down?"

She grimaced.

"Muscles stiff?"

She nodded.

He crossed the small space to her and reached up. She hesitated, then turned toward him, letting him close his hands around her waist and pull her from the saddle.

She whimpered when her toes touched the ground, and she

tightened her hands on his arms. It was his turn to grimace as he lowered her to her bottom on the ground. If he thought she'd help him gather firewood, well, it wouldn't happen tonight. She could barely bend her legs. Getting her back in the saddle tomorrow would be an endeavor.

He dropped his pack near her. "You see what we've got in there to eat. Keep in mind we've got to ration it out."

She nodded and pulled the pack toward her as he walked off to find firewood.

* * *

HE WAS REGRETTING BRINGING her already. Abigail bit her lower lip against the pain that ran all through her body, from the back of her head to the back of her heels. They'd only been on the trail a few hours—no wonder he was frustrated with her. What would she do tomorrow when they were in the saddle all day? He'd already lessened his pace out of concern for her.

She had to make herself useful or he'd send her back to the George P. Williamson Home for Wayward Girls, and she had no idea what Mrs. McBride's reaction would be. She was fairly certain the woman wouldn't accept her back to work, not after she'd run off. And she was too old to be a "wayward girl" any longer. She'd have to live outside the law as her mother had. She wondered if she had the same courage as her mother. She should start looking for it now.

With great effort, she heaved herself to her feet and tended the horses.

After arranging stones in a circle in anticipation of a fire, she laid out the supplies he'd purchased earlier and set about mixing dough for the bannocks. She hoped he was able to bring back some extra sticks that she could wrap the dough around to cook. For that matter, she hoped he could find wood to cook it over. She hadn't seen a tree for miles.

What would they do if he couldn't find wood for a fire? The desert was cold, and while they could probably eat the dried beef he'd bought, keeping warm would be a challenge.

Footsteps drew her attention, and she tensed before she caught sight of him coming up the rise.

She hadn't had much to do with men since Nate, but she knew a handsome man when she saw one, and Marshal Grey was a fine-looking man. Tall and lean, broad shouldered, long-fingered, capable hands. He had a pleasing face, lean lines, his jaw roughened by beard stubble, his lips full.

And those eyes, brilliant blue and so focused.

They fixed on her now as he approached with an arm full of twigs. Trying not to groan, she pushed to her feet to meet him. He lifted his eyebrows at her stiff movements.

"I got this," he said, and crouched next to the ring of stones to lay the sticks and start the fire.

"How is your hand?" she asked, nodding toward the bandage. She couldn't believe she'd had it in her, the violence to stab him with her fork. She'd been desperate, was the only thing. And even that had been a risk. What if he had left her in jail in town? She didn't even want to think about how alone she would have been.

He flexed his fingers. "All right."

"Do you want me to take a look at it?" She thought she should offer, though the sight of blood made her squeamish.

He lifted his gaze to hers. "You know medicine?"

She could have lied, but hadn't she already done enough of that? She shook her head.

He grunted and went back to building the fire.

She rescued two of the greener sticks and waited for the fire to die down as she wrapped the dough around the sticks.

"My mother used to make these for us when we were little. She usually had a bit of jam to sweeten it, though."

He sat next to the fire and folded his legs in front of him. "Hard to imagine Sweetheart Belle as a doting mother."

Abigail laughed roughly. "Hardly that. She did love us, in her way, but her crew was first in her thoughts."

"No anger there," he observed.

She shrugged. "No anger. It was just a way of life." As the flames from the fire he started died down, she extended the dough-wrapped sticks over them, turning so that the dough cooked evenly. "Was your mother doting?"

"Hardly that." He echoed her words. "The old man would beat the daylights out of her if she spent a minute more time with us than with him."

Abigail winced. Her mother's relationship with Joseph had been volatile, certainly, but he'd never hit her. They'd fought and snarled almost daily, but slept every night in each other's arms.

"Did you have brothers and sisters?"

"I was the oldest of four. I have a younger brother and two sisters."

Which meant he'd probably taken on a lot of responsibility, protecting his siblings. That seemed about right.

"Where are they now?"

"Back in Texas. I couldn't get out of there fast enough, but they stayed."

"I suppose none of them would rob a train."

He shook his head, a half-smile curving his lips. "As mean as my father was, he wasn't dumb enough to do that."

She wanted to defend Abe, to point out that planning a robbery and a getaway was hard, thoughtful work, but she thought the marshal probably wouldn't see it that way.

"So, ranchers? Farmers?"

"Bankers."

It was her turn to lift an eyebrow. "So bankers aren't as respectable as they want everyone to think."

"I imagine some are." He took the stick she offered him, reached for the dough and snatched his hand away when it burned his fingers. "Maybe even most."

"Maybe when we find Abe, we can send him your father's way."

He pinched a piece of his bannock off the stick. "Too late."

She stilled as she brought her own stick up. "He's dead?"

"In a bank robbery."

The words took her aback. "Oh, my heavens. Is that why you became a lawman?"

"I was already a lawman when he was killed. I caught and hung those that did it."

A chill went through her. His face betrayed no emotion. What did she really know about this man she'd attached herself to? "Have you killed a lot of men?"

He chewed on his bread and leveled a look at her. "I was a soldier, Miss Vincent."

"I didn't realize you were that old."

He gave a dry laugh. "I was fourteen. Ran away from home to join the army. Fought there at the end. Saw more than a boy should see."

"Did you go home afterwards?"

He shook his head. "Was ready to move on. I was a different person. Stronger."

She drew her legs up in front of her and wrapped her arms around them. "So killing people made you stronger."

He set his stick down, stripped bare of the bannock. "Not because I killed people, but because I took care of myself. No one was there to look out for me, show me what to do, where to go. I figured it out on my own. And I kept from getting killed myself. There's a power in that, too. Survival."

She picked up his stick and wrapped more dough around it, then held it over the fire. "Survival," she echoed.

"I think you might know something about that. I'd think even for the child of Sweetheart Belle, life wasn't easy."

She drew her legs up and wrapped her arms around them. She hadn't sat like this since she was a girl. Mrs. McBride didn't allow the girls to sit any other way than with their feet on the floor and their backs straight. Disobeying, even out of the woman's sight, was liberating. "I didn't think of it as being difficult. I had Abe, we played together, we didn't have restrictions, very few chores. I remember being paddled twice. We were happy, even with strangers coming and going, our mother coming and going. She was—she wasn't an angry person. She could be focused, but never mean. It was only when my mother died that I started thinking about running away."

His gaze sharpened. "Your stepfather?"

"His mother." She wasn't willing to tell him about Joseph. "I wasn't her blood, so I was nothing. She kept us when my mother went on her—journeys."

"That word again. Do you know how many people your mother and her crew killed?"

Her shoulders snapped tight and she almost dropped her stick into the fire. She had heard rumors about her mother from other girls at the home, once they figured out who she was.

He leaned forward, eyes narrowed. "Do you want to know?"

She should know. She should. But...she shook her head and shoved her stick into the dirt, no longer hungry. "I want to sleep now."

He grunted and stuck his own stick beside hers, still with the cooked dough on it. "A few things we need to tend to before you sleep."

He explained the parameters of the camp and where she should see to her needs. It was still dusk when she curled up in her bedroll close to the fire. But she couldn't sleep, and she knew that the marshal sat by the fire for a long while after.

* * *

MARCUS WINCED in sympathy when he glanced at Abigail sitting in her saddle. Her posture portrayed her pain, the angle of her head, the stiffness of her shoulders, the way she held her bottom off the saddle. He should take her back now. He should have taken her back yesterday. He told himself he didn't because he didn't want to take the time from the trail, which was already cold, but to be honest, she fascinated him. To have grown up with Sweetheart Belle...he couldn't imagine the life she'd led, outlaws in and out, day and night. And then she'd run off with Nate and Daniel Holland. They weren't outlaws of the same caliber of her mother, just small-time, unlucky bank robbers. He'd heard she and the younger Holland had been lovers when she had been no more than fifteen. She definitely hadn't lived the life of a lady. What surprised him was that while she was tough, she wasn't hard.

The temperature had dropped, and she huddled in her coat. They hadn't stopped for hours and he wondered if he should offer, or just continue in silence. Because of the weather, he was going to have to find better shelter tonight, or they were going to have to huddle together—or both.

He'd been avoiding that. She was so young, and hell, an outlaw's daughter, another's lover. The last person he needed to be snuggling up with.

"Hungry?" he asked.

She hesitated then shook her head.

They crested a rise and looked down onto a town that he could have sworn wasn't there his last trip through. Towns were springing up along the railroad lines all over the place. He hadn't intended to stop in a town yet since they didn't need supplies after only a night on the road, but maybe they could get a hot meal they didn't have to cook, maybe sleep in a bed.

Two beds. In two different rooms. He shifted in the saddle himself against the arousal that rose in him, that had battered him all night. He'd watched her sleep, a frown creasing her forehead against her pain. He felt like the foulest man in the world, wanting her despite that.

He didn't want to stop so early—they still had a few hours of daylight left. But he had given up his chance to sleep in a proper bed night before last and wanted to rectify that. Also, he needed to send a telegram to the marshal's office to apprise them of his progress.

"You're not going to tell them who I am, are you?"

He angled his head to look at her. "Why would I do that?"

"I'm Sweetheart Belle's daughter." She swallowed. "I haven't been her daughter in a long time, if you know what I mean. People used to make a point of mentioning it, you know."

"She's been gone a long time."

"I don't think people forget."

"I won't tell anyone who you are," he said, and nudged his horse down the hill.

He left Abigail sitting on her horse outside the hotel when he went in to secure the rooms. Damn if she wasn't costing him a pretty penny. The proprietor looked at Marcus then out the window at Abigail, who was tending to the horses. Now, Marcus could tell right away she was a woman despite the hat and layered shirts. The curve of her ass in those jeans gave her away. But he didn't know if the proprietor saw it.

If he did notice, Marcus would say she was his prisoner and take her upstairs. He hoped he didn't have to stick with that story, though, because he didn't want to have to keep an eye on her every minute.

He paid, made an appointment to use the services of the bath house then went out to fetch Abigail.

"Avoid the proprietor, if you can. He has an eye on you."

She nodded. "Where are you going?"

"Checking in at the sheriff's office."

She frowned, but nodded and took her satchel into the hotel.

He ambled down the fresh lumber boardwalk and down to the sheriff's office. The place was just as new as the boardwalk outside, the scent of the raw lumber tickling his nose. The bars of the jail cell in the back were shiny. Marcus wondered if it had been put to use yet. Unlikely if the sheriff sat inside waiting for crime to come to him.

The man behind the desk, not so new, looked up from the dime novel he was reading, and scowled when he saw the star on Marcus's coat. "Help you?"

"Just checking in. On the trail of a couple of train robbers. They hit a train in New Mexico, shot some of the railroad men, and took off back east. Have any strangers come through?"

The sheriff shook his head, his expression unchanging. "Heard about a bank robbery in Padilla, though." He pronounced it Pad-ill-a. "Couple fellas. Said they looked Indian."

The hairs on the back of Marcus's neck rose. "Anyone hurt?"

"Clerk got a pistol alongside the head."

Marcus's senses went on high alert. "Older man, and a young one?"

The sheriff nodded toward a board filled with pictures. "Got the flyer right over there."

Marcus gave the book a pointed look. "You don't think they'll come for your bank next?"

"Why should they? We don't have payroll showing up for a few weeks yet. Ain't nothing in there for them." He picked up his book again. "You here long?"

Marcus crossed to the board and studied the crude drawings of the wanted poster. "You mind if I take these?"

"Help yourself."

Marcus yanked the flyers off the nails and wondered what Abigail would think of what her brother had become. He'd never had that thought while pursuing a fugitive.

He strode into the hotel and up the stairs, past the startled proprietor. His boots hit the fresh wood floor with measured strides, and he banged on the door of the room he'd given Abigail only once before it swung open and she stared up at him.

"What is it?"

"We're not staying." Unwilling to have the conversation in the hall, he stepped inside and closed the door before showing her the pictures. "Do you know them?"

Lifting her hands slowly, she took the papers from him, studying one, then the other. "This is Joseph." But that one she hardly looked at. She was staring at the sketch of her brother.

"Is that Abe?"

She nodded slowly, not blinking. "He's so grown up." Finally she looked up at him. "They robbed a bank?"

"Just the two of them, near as I can tell. And just three days ago. So we're going to Padilla to see what leads we can find." He took a step back. He should leave her here, have the sheriff see her home. But what if Mrs. McBride wouldn't take her back in? Where would she end up? He didn't want to be responsible for her ending up in a brothel, or worse.

So he'd take her with him.

"Get your things. We're heading out."

That meant riding in the dark, but he thought they'd be okay for a bit. Padilla was down the railroad a little bit.

"Why would they rob a bank after robbing a train? Does that make sense? Especially if they are already being pursued?"

"I couldn't tell you. But we're going to Padilla to find out."

She nodded and turned to shove her belongings back into the leather satchel. His gaze drifted past her to the new bed with its white linens. Seemed he was cursed to never sleep in a bed again.

"We need to get you a new bag," he muttered as he followed her down the stairs.

She pulled the valise against her. "This was my mother's."

He frowned. "It's not good for horseback."

"I can't leave it behind."

He didn't have time to argue. But as he took the lead and crossed to the stable to see about getting fresh horses, he wondered how he got saddled with a sentimental girl. He should have left her back in Fortune.

But in a matter of minutes, he'd arranged for rested horses, saddled them, and they were on their way to Padilla.

They made good progress while it was light, but lightning to the south of them was just one more message that this quest was cursed.

Fat raindrops started falling after sundown, and Marcus handed his oilcloth slicker over to Abigail. He hadn't thought to get her one, and the last thing he needed was for her to get sick and slow him down further.

The rain picked up, falling steadily, and ran in his face, blurring his vision. To continue would be too dangerous. He had to find a shelter.

A few miles down, he did, a shack near the railroad. He grabbed Abigail's reins and turned her to follow him. He urged her inside and took his slicker from her so he could see to the horses. No shelter for them, but he was able to feed them under the overhang of the roof so their food wouldn't get wet.

"What is this place?" Abigail asked when he rejoined her inside the shack.

He shrugged and peeled off his wet shirt, aware only after the fact that she was staring at his bared chest in the dim light. The hell with that. He wasn't going to catch pneumonia to save her sensibilities. After all, she'd ridden with Nate Holland and been his lover. Marcus wasn't the first naked man she'd seen.

He dropped to the floor and tugged off his boots and set them by the door. "You should probably do the same. No fun putting on wet boots."

She did, looking longingly at the empty pot-bellied stove.

"Wood's too wet," he said. "Unless there's some already in there."

She shook her head. "I already looked."

He grunted. Just his luck. He stood again and unbuckled his belt. He would be cold as hell in his long johns, but better than shivering in wet clothes.

Even his damn bedroll was wet, but he spread it on the floor and stretched on top of it. At least it was too dark for Abigail to see the rise of his cock when she copied his movements and lay down beside him.

When they got to the next town, maybe he should seek the company of one of the saloon girls so he wasn't always thinking about parting Abigail's legs. He turned away, curling in on himself to try to warm himself.

And heard her teeth chattering.

Of course.

He flopped onto his back and sighed. "Turn on your side."

"What?"

"The only way to keep warm is for me to put my arms around you. Turn on your side."

* * *

ABIGAIL GAVE a shiver that had nothing to do with being cold and for a moment considered refusing. But she was so cold she could barely think and did as he asked.

His skin, when he touched hers, was icy, and she had a pang of guilt. He was so cold because he'd given her his coat. So she held herself stiff when he looped his arm over her body and drew her against his chest.

His naked chest. In the dim lantern light, she'd seen the muscular contours of his chest and the sprinkling of wiry hair. All the dormant desires she'd buried when she moved to the home for wayward girls bounced back to life at the sight of him.

And now his strong arm was across her, holding her against him.

"You're cold."

"Give it a minute," he replied, his voice gruff.

She was grateful she still wore her shirt, a barrier between her skin and his. He wore his long johns, rough against the backs of her bare thighs.

And then his hips nestled into hers and she felt his hardening sex prod against her bottom. She stiffened in response.

"I'm not going to hurt you." But his voice was even rougher than before.

She believed him—he'd made a point of seeing to her comfort, even at the expense of his own. She didn't think he would take advantage of her vulnerability. He was a man of integrity.

And she was Sweetheart Belle's daughter, and Nate Holland's former lover. All she could think of was the press of his sex against her bottom, and the heat that was rolling through her, chasing the chill. She shifted and he grunted, almost like he was in pain. He closed his hand over her hip, easing her away, just a little.

"Do you have a skirt, or something, you could use to cover your legs?" he asked.

"Everything in my satchel is as soaked as my clothes."

He grunted again then pulled her back fully against him. He was warmer now, and his cock stretched to the small of her back. She could feel the hammering of his heart, and his breath came hot against the side of her neck. She recognized the reaction.

She wanted to relax against him, wanted to explore the sensations he aroused in her. But she didn't know how he'd respond. Would he think her a whore if she leaned into him?

She didn't want that. So she held herself stiffly until she felt his breathing even out as he fell into sleep.

* * *

HER SKIN WAS SO soft beneath his hand as he smoothed it over her leg, from her knee to her curvy bottom. He hadn't been with a woman in so long, and she pressed back against him with a moan of appreciation. He glided his hand from her bottom, under her shirt, finding her breast, rubbing his thumb beneath her nipple, which hardened at his touch. He drew in a breath as she turned to him, wrapped one hand around the back of his neck and dragged the other down his chest to wrap around his cock through his long johns. The rough fabric added a sensation that had him gritting his teeth and pumping into her fist as she rubbed the length of him in an experienced rhythm.

He turned his head into her neck, dragging his lips along the delicate line of her throat that had been driving him crazy all day. He cupped the weight of her breast fully in his hand. Moaning, she arched her back, stroking him in a more determined fashion. He closed his eyes to savor the lust running through him. He was no longer cold.

He felt something different, a tugging near his thigh, and opened his eyes to see her hand slip between her legs, stroking her own sex. The scent of her arousal wrapped around him, and he pushed her hand away from his cock to push down his long johns, reason fleeing in his desire to be deep inside her heat, to feel her pussy squeeze around him.

He stopped himself, fisting his own cock now, stroking himself to a frenzy, fascinated by the play of her hand over her sex, her knowledge of her own body. Her breathing hitched and sighed, the slick sounds of her fingers against her pussy growing more frantic, until her hips bucked.

He could hold back no longer. He came in long pulses that jerked his whole body with the force.

And when he opened his eyes this time, she was asleep on her side, her clothes in place, her hands folded under her cheek.

Good Lord. She was making him crazy, having dreams like he hadn't had since he was a boy. He rolled to his feet and went outside to wash.

* * *

THE MARSHAL certainly was surly this morning. He'd barely said two words to her since she woke up, and they'd eaten a couple of biscuits saved from yesterday. Then he'd gone outside into the watery light of the post-storm morning to saddle the horses, only summoning her with a brusque, "Come on," when he was ready to go.

The ground was muddy, and mist still hung in the air after the storm, but it wasn't as cold as yesterday, thanks to the humidity. She hoped they could reach Padilla today and possibly stay the night in a proper bed, with blankets and maybe a fire. She'd never been so cold as she'd been last night, though the marshal's body had warmed her enough to fall asleep, and sleep deeply.

She wondered what had him in a bad mood. He had a lead on her brother and Joseph and it wasn't raining, though the mud slowed the horses down.

"Did you not sleep well?" she ventured.

He slanted a look at her. "I did not."

"I'm sorry for that."

His nostrils flared. "Hardly your fault."

"Maybe we'll get a room tonight?"

He scowled. "You had a room, didn't you? Back at the home for wayward girls? Warm, with a bed and blankets and warm meals?"

She flushed. "I'm not going to leave my brother to my mother's fate."

"He hasn't given a damn about you for how many years?"

She flinched. Why was he being so cruel? The words were true, yes, and sliced deeper because of it. "He's only fifteen. He hasn't seen me since he was a boy." And she was sure Joseph didn't make an effort to encourage contact.

"You shouldn't have come."

She understood that he was as upset with himself for allowing her to come as he was with her. "Are you going to leave me in the next town?"

"Thinking about it."

"Mrs. McBride won't take me back after I ran away. It's a rule in the house."

"You work there, you aren't one of the girls."

"The rules remain the same. If you send me home, I won't have any options."

"You should have thought of that before you left."

He nudged his horse into a canter, sending mud flying up to hit her thigh. She watched him, a bit off-balance in the saddle as her horse struggled with his footing, but then she leaned forward, urging her horse to follow.

Padilla was a bit bigger than the last town, a little more established, the false fronts of the store weathered, the boardwalks warped. There was a livery near the end of town, a depot, and two hotels.

Marcus left her with the horses outside the hotel, and when he returned, his mouth was grim.

"What is it?"

"Nosy clerk. Just so you know, we're married."

CHAPTER 3

She stared. "Married?"

"The clerk was asking too many questions. It was all I could think of to satisfy her."

"You could have told her I was your prisoner."

He lifted his gaze to her then, and his nostrils flared. "You really want to spend the night in a jail cell?" He nodded toward the brick building at the other end of town. "You think you're better off there?"

"No, of course not." But what did it mean, they had to pretend they were married?

"I'll see to the horses. She'll show you to the room." He dropped his bedroll on her shoulder and handed her the satchel. Then without another word, he took the horses' reins and led them down to the livery.

She took a deep breath and walked—well, staggered—into the hotel.

"Your husband ordered a bath for you," the woman, probably close to the marshal's age, said as she led the way up the stairs. "How long have you been on the road?"

"Only a few days, but we were caught in a storm last night. A hot bath sounds wonderful."

Would he give her privacy while she enjoyed it?

"I'll send a boy up with the tub and hot water."

"Did my husband—" she choked on the word, "order a bath for himself?"

"He said he'd go to the bath house, but he didn't want to subject you to such roughness."

A bath house. She wondered if he'd then go to a saloon and find a girl. She didn't understand the shaft of jealous heat that shot through her. He wasn't her real husband, only pretend.

She became aware the other woman was looking at her through her eyelashes, and blushed. Was the clerk thinking the same thing?

"You're much younger than he is. Have you been married long?"

Abigail stammered. She should have asked Marcus to elaborate on the ruse. What if this woman caught them out in a lie? "Not long. A few months."

"Then I wouldn't be too worried." She opened the door to a room at the front of the hotel, with a window overlooking the street, but Abigail didn't pay attention to that. Instead she stared at the wide bed with white sheets in the center of the room, and swallowed.

She'd been Nate Holland's lover, so she wasn't a stranger to men and their desires. But Marcus was so different from Nate, a man, not a boy, and though he clearly desired her, he had held himself in check. Would he still, when he saw that bed?

She let his bedroll fall to the floor and set her valise on the chair beside the chest of drawers.

"Is there anything else you need?" the woman asked, standing just outside the room with her hand on the doorknob.

Abigail shook her head, unsure of what to say.

"I'll send up the bath, and a little food. Dinner won't be served until seven."

Time—it seemed like weeks since she'd had to think about what time it was. In reality, it had just been since she'd joined the marshal.

Once the woman left, Abigail wandered to the window to look down on the town.

The streets were muddy and churned up from the rain and horse traffic. From where she stood, she could count three saloons, a bank, the sheriff's office and two general stores.

The day was still gray, but she could see the break in the clouds to the west where the sun was setting, sending out a watery light. If the sun was out tomorrow, traveling wouldn't be such a challenge.

She was wondering where the marshal was when the knock on the door startled her. She crossed the room to let the boy in with her tub. He set it by the fire silently then retreated with the promise of water. She sat on the edge of the bed to remove her boots and wiggled her toes, sighing at the freedom. She wished she had clean clothes to wear after her bath.

The boy returned with one bucket of warm water, which barely filled the bottom of the tub. She waited impatiently for him to bring more water, and when she was finally alone, she stripped and stepped into the steaming water. She almost sobbed with pleasure as the heat seeped into her skin. She sank back and hoped the marshal didn't return soon.

* * *

"It was the damnedest thing," the sheriff drawled, circling his glass on the wooden bar in front of him.

Marcus had located the man in the saloon, paying particular attention to one of the saloon girls. The man, maybe five years older than Marcus, had scowled when Marcus claimed his attention. But now he was fully into sharing the story.

"It was like they didn't have a plan, didn't even have fresh horses. The poor horses were blowing hard and lathered when the men came out of the bank, and honest to God, I don't know how my posse didn't catch up to them afterwards. Damn horses probably went lame." He signaled for another drink. "I hate to see people mistreat animals."

"But it was just the two of them."

The sheriff shook his head as the bartender set the glass in front of him. "Three. One about your age, a blond man and a scrawny kid, taller than the others, but a stiff breeze would blow him away. Older guy cuffed him on the head a couple of times, that I saw."

A third man. He wondered why his picture hadn't been among the flyers. Who was it? "Why didn't you shoot them? You seemed to have spent a good amount of time observing them."

"Wasn't that much time. And I ain't going to shoot a kid."

Marcus had to wonder if the sheriff didn't spend most of his time sitting in the saloon, where they were now, and may not have been able to get off a shot without hitting an innocent bystander.

"Where did your posse lose them?"

"North of here, there's a river, and then a mountain. Like I said, I don't know how they outran us on those horses. They must know the area pretty well, and frankly, when it got dark, I didn't want my men out there. A horse could easily turn a hoof or something, and have to be put down." He took a sip of his whiskey. "That was the one thing they did right, plan the robbery late in the day so we couldn't track them in the dark."

"Sounds like that's not all they did right." Marcus rose and put money on the bar for his drink and the sheriff's. "Can we get someone tomorrow to show us where you lost them?"

"I can, but you aren't going to find them, not this long after the robbery. They're probably long gone."

Frustration tore at him. If this man hadn't given up, had gone back the following day, Joseph and Abe might already be in custody. "Unless those horses went lame and they're stranded out there. I'd appreciate a guide. We want to leave at first light."

Without waiting for a response, he pushed through the swinging doors and headed for the bath house.

A short time later, with most of the trail mud washed away, he headed upstairs. He hated bath houses, but the stop was a necessary evil, especially when there was a woman in his room.

A woman pretending to be his wife.

He pushed his hand through his still-damp hair. He'd managed to keep that thought at the back of his mind all evening, but now he was about to come face to face with it. Last night, holding her in his arms had been pure hell. He'd never slept beside a woman, and hadn't expected the torture his arousal visited upon him.

He stepped into the room and froze in his tracks.

Abigail stared up at him with wide eyes from the tub where she sat, naked.

His gaze flicked to the curve of her breasts that rose above the water, though her nipples were hidden by her drawn-up legs.

Naked, pretty, drawn-up legs. His palm itched to run over the smooth flesh.

He dragged his gaze back to her face. "You're still in the bath," he said dumbly.

"I fell asleep."

Her voice was husky, and the sound of it, the sultriness of a woman awakening, the heat of the room, all of it curled around him, held him in place in the doorway.

"Can you hand me the drying sheet?"

Her words weren't as slow, but her request took a moment to process. Handing her the towel would require him moving closer to her, and he wasn't sure he had the self-control not to touch all that soft, pale skin if he did.

Damn, she was pretty, dark hair piled on her head, loose strands clinging to the damp skin of her neck. The line of her shoulders, the indentation of her spine, features he'd never noticed on another woman. Why was he noticing now, when he couldn't act on the lust pooling in his belly?

She turned to look at him, leaning over the edge of the tub, one arm folded on the edge, the other draped over, graceful, inviting.

Grinding his teeth, he took two steps backwards and closed the door between them.

Back in the saloon, he eyed the girls who moved from one man to another, promising sweet sin. He studied their faces beneath the heavy make-up they wore, and saw Abigail in every one.

He should take advantage of that, slake his lust for her on one of these women, but he knew that wouldn't do. He'd indulged in saloon girls before and always come away unsatisfied. Oh, he'd ejaculated, the women had made sure of that, but something from the experience was missing.

"Good evening, Marshal."

He looked up into the darkly kohled eyes of one of the girls. Her dark hair was like Abigail's, and she was around the same age, but the similarity ended there. Her corset pushed her breasts so high that he could see a hint of nipple, and below the corset, her skirt was hitched up, hinting at easy access to pleasure, showing off her short, curvy legs.

She took his inspection as invitation and sat on the barstool beside him, placing her hand high on his thigh. His cock twitched, but not as eagerly as it had for Abigail.

"It's been a long time since I entertained a lawman," she said in a low voice. "Want to come up and show me how your cuffs work?"

He chuckled and laid a coin on the counter for his drink before rising. "I don't think I will, if it's all the same." As hard as it was, he was returning to the hotel, to his "wife."

Abigail was in bed when he opened the door, her back to him, but he could see in the dim light coming through the thin curtains that she wore a gown of some sort. The sweet, clean scent of her filled the room, and he wanted to bury his face in her neck and breathe her in.

Crossing the room was a mistake. Toeing off his boots and shucking his clothes to climb in beside her was a mistake, but he did it anyway, the sheets cool against his skin. He shifted, just a little, toward the warmth of her body.

He could have been a gentleman and slept on the floor, but damn it, he'd been denied a bed once on this trip, and he was paying for it. He might as well get the comfort of it.

Only lying stiffly on his side, studying the curve of her neck and shoulder, imagining what her body looked like beneath the thin cotton of her gown, was not as comfortable as he'd imagined. His cock strained against the wool of his long johns, as if it was trying to reach her from across the bed. The pounding of his own pulse was slowly driving him mad, and he was debating returning to the saloon just to find release when Abigail turned to face him.

God, she was pretty with those deep-set eyes, wide cheekbones, full lips. He curved his hand around her head and kissed her, slanting his mouth over hers.

Instead of protesting, as she should have done, she cupped her hand over his and opened for him like a flower seeking rain.

Her full lips were soft, and moved against his reflexively. He'd never kissed a woman who kissed him back, her hand releasing his before threading through his hair, holding him to her. He couldn't stop himself from slipping his tongue inside, gliding along hers, which made her sigh and nestle closer to him. She tasted like sleep and a hint of sage. He curved his hand over her waist and brought her fully against him, breasts to chest, core to erection. Instead of shying away, she softened against him, sweet and giving.

He'd never had a woman offer him anything without wanting something in return. That alone should have made him break away, but her nipples hardened against his chest. Heat sparked through him like rock on flint. All sense left his head to speed south, taking up residence in his cock.

She was no virgin. She'd been Nate Holland's lover, maybe Daniel Holland's, too. She had brought herself on this journey, she was in his bed, her body pressed wantonly against his. He fisted his fingers in the soft lawn of her gown, intent on drawing it up, on plunging into her, copying the rhythm their mouths had found until he exploded inside her.

Her soft sigh of pleasure when his tongue stroked just so brought him to his senses. He lifted his head, breaking the kiss, though her fingers still twined in his hair. Her eyes drifted open dreamily and she smiled.

That smile had the effect of an explosion in his chest, and he slid backwards off the bed, losing a few strands of hair by the root when she didn't release him right away.

"I'll sleep on the floor," he muttered, rising and reaching for his bedroll.

"Marshal. There's no need."

Her tone was chiding, and not sultry anymore, but breathy. God help him if that didn't arouse him more, thinking of her breath on his skin—his chest, his stomach, lower. If he returned to the bed, to her arms, he'd lose his honor.

He should go to the barn, put more distance between them, but he couldn't bring himself to leave the warmth of the room. He didn't look at her as he spread his bedroll, but in his mind's eye, he saw her on her side on the bed, the sheet pooled at her hips, her lips swollen, her eyes dark with desire.

Finally, he heard her shift on the mattress, draw the covers over her and breathe out a long sigh.

He stretched onto his back, his hands folded on his stomach, and stared at the ceiling, wondering why his usual iron will was not strong enough when it came to her.

* * *

FEENEY, the man from the posse the sheriff had sent to escort them, was older, thin white hair flipping up beneath the brim of his hat and a sparse white beard hanging from leathery cheeks. He met them in front of the hotel at first light, and welcomed the breakfast Marcus purchased in the dining room. Afterwards, he practically had to drag the old man back to his horse, which plodded along at a pace that made Marcus shift in his saddle like a child in church. If this was Feeney's usual pace, Marcus had no question about how the bank robbers had escaped, even with tired horses.

He shifted in the saddle and exchanged a look with Abigail, whose tight shoulders and lifted reins conveyed that she was just as impatient as he was.

The old man regaled them with a detailed account of the pursuit as they rode.

"Saw 'em run out of the bank from my place next to the smithy," Feeney said, his words as slow as his horse's steps. "The big one had a bag in his hand and vaulted onto a horse. The white one, he had his pistol waving, catching the sunlight, and was hollering as if he wanted everyone to know what they'd done. The skinny one lifted his rifle, aiming at anyone who might come out the door behind them, before he mounted his own horse and followed the big one down Main Street, hell-for-leather. Pardon, ma'am."

"No shots were fired?" Marcus asked, trying not to notice the pretty smile Abigail gave the older man.

41

Feeney noticed, though, and straightened in his saddle, adjusting his hat on his head as if he was riding in the presence of the Queen of England.

"Feeney? No shots?" Marcus repeated.

Feeney scowled. "No shots. But as soon as they left, the clerk came running out, saying how's they'd been robbed, and to call the sheriff. I sent my apprentice to get the sheriff and went to saddle my brave Miranda." He patted his roan's neck. "She's been through hell and back with me, running from Comanches and scalawags."

Running *from*, Marcus thought. Not running *after*. "How many men pursued them?"

"Seven of us, counting myself and the sheriff, without a thought to our own safety." He'd turned his attention back to Abigail and smiled, showing yellowed teeth.

Abigail returned the smile, and Marcus saw no artifice in it. The old man appeared dazzled, his gaze riveted to her.

"What's a pretty young lady like yourself doing out here chasing outlaws?" Feeney asked her.

"Feeney." Marcus redirected the man's thoughts. He'd play up the lie that they were married if he had to, but he really hated to lie. "How far behind was the posse?"

"I couldn't say. Not a good deal. We were surprised to see them on the road ahead of us. I'm thinking they didn't know the area well, or they wouldn't have stuck to the road where we could find them."

"What did you intend to do if you caught them?" Abigail asked, a little breathless.

"Well, hang them, ma'am."

She shivered. Marcus wondered if the old man noticed that she was a shade paler than before.

"I haven't seen any trees," she pointed out.

"We have ways, ma'am," Feeney said.

Marcus didn't press to find out what they were.

Marcus kept his horse behind Abigail and Feeney, who fell into conversation about the land and its history. Feeney seemed to know every outlaw who'd ever set up camp in New Mexico Territory.

"Did you ever hear of Sweetheart Belle?" Abigail asked, and Marcus went stiff.

"Heard of her?" Feeney's laugh rang out over the flat land. "I met her once. She was in a saloon, drinking men under the table, playing a hand of cards. They let me in the game, and I was so taken by her beauty, I lost every dime I had, and didn't regret a minute of it. I heard she was shot in the breast. Seems such a shame. Beautiful breasts."

Feeney drew up his horse before Marcus could protest his choice of topic.

"We got as far as there."

He pointed to a dip in the trail that Marcus realized was a riverbed.

"Once they crossed the river, well, we lost them. Didn't care to cross, as swollen as it was from the rains. Was amazed, truth be told, that the water didn't take any of them under, tired as their horses were."

"Which way did they go once they got to the other side?"

"Straight on up that way."

Marcus followed the old man's gesture, squinting across the river at the rocky trail that angled steeply up the mountain. "I thought their mounts were tired. And you couldn't catch them?"

"Didn't cross the river. Sheriff said it's not his county anymore."

Marcus huffed out a breath and picked up his reins. If the man had crossed jurisdictional lines, Marcus wouldn't be out here in the cold. The sheriff had certainly been justified to do so.

Marcus looked at Abigail again, then back to Feeney. "Any other way across this river?"

"Sure, there's a bridge about five miles or so down. River's not too deep now, though. Been a few days since the rains."

Marcus scowled. "I guess you wouldn't know, since you didn't cross it."

The man appeared affronted. "I've crossed it before."

"I can cross," Abigail interjected.

He shot her a look. "You will not, until I determine it's safe." He had to risk it, because going to find the bridge and doubling back would cost them a day they couldn't afford. But if it was too dangerous for Abigail, he'd send her back to town with Feeney.

He urged his horse forward, and the animal shook his head when his foot touched the frigid water.

If it got too deep, he'd have to lose the day or risk hypothermia. He nudged the horse's sides and, head down, the animal headed deeper into the water, which hadn't yet reached the bottoms of Marcus's boots. He turned back at about the halfway point to look at Abigail, only to discover she had followed him into the river.

His first instinct was to wheel his horse and chase her back to the far bank, but he didn't want to keep his horse in the water any longer than necessary. Anger at her disobedience burned in him, but he couldn't act on it, not when they were both in danger.

"Take off your boots!" he called over his shoulder. "You'll need them dry when you get to the other side. And make sure your satchel is out of the water." He hoped his own bedroll stayed above the surface, because it would never dry before tonight.

He wanted to wait for her and guide her horse across, because damn, what if her horse lost its footing and dumped her in the water?

"Can you swim?"

"I can."

But her voice was shaky, and he looked at the eddies rushing around his horse's legs. His horse shifted impatiently and Marcus gave the animal its head, praying that Abigail could keep her seat, and that the river didn't get any deeper.

The current pushed his mount down the river. He kept his attention on the bank, and damn, it looked steeper the farther he drifted. He lifted his reins and urged the horse against the flow, to where the bank was lower. Every line of his body was tense, and he looked over his shoulder to see Abigail following, her concentration on her horse's neck. Beyond her, their guide watched, shaking his head.

For a moment, his horse floundered and he thought he'd be going into the drink. But the horse found his footing and pressed toward the bank. As his horse angled up, picking up the pace as he emerged from the water, Marcus looked back.

Abigail continued on, grim-faced, her hands firm on the reins. He let his horse carry him onto the bank and dismounted, waiting to go into the water if Abigail needed him.

But she didn't. Her hands were steady as she guided her horse beside him. She dropped her boots and her satchel to the ground and slid from her saddle and into his arms.

He absorbed her into him, wrapping her tightly against his chest, feeling her shaking. Relief rolled through him like the icy water behind them, and he fought to keep his feet.

Finally, she lifted her head and looked up at him with a grin that surprised him. "We made it."

Jesus. "You need a minute?" Because he did.

She looked at the trail. "We should go."

He studied her a minute, wondering if her bravery was real or for him. He decided to take advantage of it and held the reins as she took a couple of attempts to get back in the saddle. She was laughing by the time she landed and took the reins from him. He swung into his saddle, his own legs shaky, and led the way up the trail.

CHAPTER 4

They ate in the saddle, stopping only to relieve themselves behind the sparse bushes on the way up the mountain. She remembered this area from her childhood, remembered the hide-out was in a canyon, but not precisely where.

They hadn't spoken about their kiss last night, and how she'd wanted more. She didn't know if people talked about such things. Riding in silence, however, nagged at her.

Maybe she shouldn't have been so bold. He already didn't want her along on this journey. He'd kissed her, yes, but she could have feigned outrage instead of kissing him back, instead of pressing into him, rubbing against him, playing the wanton. Perhaps he would have preferred that. Perhaps...

She didn't have romantic notions, really. She didn't think he'd take her away from the home, make her an honest woman. She wanted to see what sex with him would be like, sex with a real man, not a boy.

"When I was fourteen, I ran away with Nate Holland."

His gaze snapped to her face. "I knew that."

He did? How much did he know? But his expression gave none of that away.

"He came to my house and was so sweet to me, when not many were. He'd take me to the barn and kiss me and make me feel so good. I gave him my virginity there in the hay, my skirts around my waist." What a disappointment it had been. His cock had not fulfilled the promise his hands and mouth had made to her body. "When he left, I went with him. Wasn't long before we were rutting all the time, out in the open, day, night, didn't matter. He was crazy about me."

Marcus was watching her now, and she couldn't hold his gaze, so started twisting the reins. "If I hadn't left with him, Abe might be okay. I didn't give my brother a second thought when I left. I just wanted to be happy."

"Were you?"

She blew out a breath and let the reins unfold. "It was exciting, but terrifying. Nate and Daniel wanted to hold up banks, and they'd use me as a distraction. I never went in a bank with them, but I sure enough helped." She looked up at him. "When they arrested Nate and Daniel, that's when they sent me to the George P. Williamson Home for Wayward Girls. I wasn't quite sixteen."

"You were with him a good while, then."

"I've not always made the best choices," she admitted. "I know you don't want me here with you. But I can be of use, I promise, when we get to Abe. Until then." She rode a little closer and touched his thigh. "I wouldn't mind if you wanted to kiss me some more. Or even if you wanted to spread my legs." She had a feeling rutting with Marcus would be far more pleasurable than with Nate. Marcus had already shown a great deal of self control on their nights together. Maybe, if he emptied himself inside her, he wouldn't be so tight all the time.

* * *

Marcus delayed finding a campsite as long as possible, her words playing in his head over and over. All he could think about was spreading her legs, looking upon her, pushing into her soft heat.

He should have set her straight, chided her for her bold talk, let her know in no uncertain terms that such a condition was off the table.

Except his control was slipping and he couldn't be certain he wouldn't kiss her again, wouldn't want to touch her. He told himself he could resist her better out here in the open than in the warmth of a bed.

She was slumped in the saddle, exhausted, when he found the shelter of a rock overhang. The natural barricade blocked the cool wind and had clearly been used as a camp before, if the circle of rocks was an indication. He wondered momentarily if the previous campers had been his quarry.

He dismounted and crossed to help Abigail from her saddle. She rested her hands on his shoulders as he closed his about her waist and lifted her. She swung her legs over and glided down the length of his body, leaning into him, her sleepy eyes suddenly conveying a different message. Every instinct told him to let her go, to push her away, but he held her just a little closer, the heat of her body seeping into his, his swelling cock a breath from her belly, just enough to make him crazy with wanting.

She stood there, her hands not moving, her eyes on him, letting this hell play out in his body. A smile curved her lips, the sultry cant of it giving him just enough courage to back away.

"Get the bedrolls ready," he said gruffly. "I'll see to the horses and look for wood for the fire."

In the end, there was no wood for the fire, and very little light with the thick cloud cover overhead diffusing what little light the moon provided. But when he returned to camp to tell her they were eating dried beef for dinner, he found she'd placed the bedrolls together, no space between them. With blankets on top, it looked for all the world like a marriage bed, and his heart hitched, just the way it did when he faced off with an outlaw.

He'd thought he had a good handle on his desire, but it sprang back to life at the sight.

"No wood?" she asked, unlacing her boots.

He shook his head and sat with a grunt onto the end of his bedroll. "Going to be cold tonight. You might want to keep your boots on, or at least stuff something in them so critters don't take up residence."

She gave a little laugh and passed him a couple of biscuits she must have gotten from the hotel this morning. He wolfed them down and washed the thickness down with a few swigs from his canteen. She then handed over some dried beef, anticipating him.

"Did you eat?" he asked, narrowing his eyes.

"There's enough," she said, lifting an edge of the blanket and slipping beneath.

He wished he'd waited to tend the horses, that he had some excuse to get up and away from her. His pulse raced, his own heartbeat drowning out his good sense as he followed her beneath the blankets.

He could have kept to the far side of the bedroll, but he didn't, seeking the warmth of her body, curving himself around her back and bringing her close. She gave a little sigh and a little wiggle, and the last grip on his control fled.

He eased her onto her back and kissed her, his tongue stroking deeply into her willing mouth while her hands moved over his shoulders and into his hair. His elbow brushed her breast, and he felt it give beneath the rough fabric of her shirt. Nothing would do but that he touched her.

When he covered her breast with his palm, they both groaned. She shifted to move closer to his cock, rubbing her belly against him.

He should pull away. He was responsible for her. He couldn't allow this to happen. But he just had to—

He slid his hand over her belly and cupped her mons through her denims, rubbing lightly, drawing a whimper of pleasure from her. Damn, she was hot, and he could already imagine her wrapped around his cock, squeezing him. He rubbed, and she rubbed back, her breath growing shallow. He lifted his head to look at her, to watch her face as he shoved the fabric down and parted her silky curls with his fingers, stroking through them, wriggling his hand deeper into them until he coated his fingers in her juices, sliding them over her tender skin.

Her eyes widened as he found the nub of nerves that made her whole body go tight, made her pump her hips against his hand. Her shudders shook the whole bed as he held her on the precipice of her climax. He pressed her legs open further and stroked with just his fingertips, up and down.

The scent of her arousal filled his nostrils, and his cock wept, aching for the opportunity to slide into her sweet pussy.

And then she came, bucking her hips so hard she almost dislodged his touch, her hard little nub softening beneath his fingers as her release washed over him.

Good God, she was even wetter now as she sank back onto the bedroll, a smile of pleasure on her relaxed face.

He should bolt, he should leave, sleep elsewhere. But just as he found the willpower, she wrapped her fingers around his cock through the opening of his fly.

Just the feel of her flesh on his nearly sent him over the edge, and then when she started to stroke, long, sure caresses from the base of his shaft to the head, he lost all will to leave. He rolled onto his back to give her greater access and watched as she worked his cock, her head tilted as she studied her efforts.

She levered herself between his legs, kneeling with her shirt askew, baring one breast—he hadn't remembered unbuttoning it. Had she? She studied his cock with some concentration as she fisted him, and then lowered her mouth to the tip of it, her tongue flicking out to glide across his skin.

His hips shot off the bedroll. "What—? How do you know about that?"

She pushed her loosened hair back from her face and gave him a slanted smile. "I grew up in an immodest household, and then was sent to a school for wayward girls who liked to talk about their sins. Do you like it?"

He'd never experienced it before, never trusted a whore enough to perform the deed. Could he trust Abigail? Lust overwhelmed common sense. He needed to bury himself in her heat, and she was willing. He lifted his hips again.

She parted her lips around him, her gaze on his. The heat from her mouth was incredible, and he hung onto control by his fingernails.

She advanced the length of him, her lips tight around his shaft, and then her tongue slid against his flesh, supple and sweet. Amazement chased desire as she took him completely, her tongue tracing the thick veins of his cock, stroking against the base of him, just above his balls. The head of him bumped the back of her throat and his body went rigid as he gave over to pure sensation.

She slid her mouth up his length and down, tongue curling and dancing as if giving him pleasure gave her pleasure. Her nails dug into his thigh as she rose and descended in an imitation of sex. He wished for more light so he could watch her face, watch his cock disappear into her mouth.

His balls tightened at the image, and he was lost, his orgasm ripping from him and into her mouth in long, hot spurts.

He couldn't tell who was more disappointed, her or himself, when she sat up and wiped the corners of her lips.

"Is that it?" she asked, studying his flagging cock.

None of that should have happened, but just now he couldn't work up any regret. He pulled her against him, his hand on her breast as she lay beside him.

"For now. We're getting started at first light."

And he fell into a deep sleep.

* * *

ABIGAIL LAY on her side in the dim morning light and studied the tent in the blankets made by Marcus's cock. It was hard again, even though he was asleep. The prodding heat of it had awakened her.

Last night had been surprising and pleasurable, but something was missing. She'd felt delicious with his fingers stroking her, but had felt empty of the same sensation she felt when she explored her own body. She missed the sensation of a cock inside her, and the curiosity of what Marcus would feel like between her legs was driving her mad.

She stroked her fingertips lightly along the exposed length of him and watched him twitch. He'd enjoyed her mouth last night, but would he want to wake to find himself buried deep inside her?

She had to know.

She stripped off her britches and tossed them aside, ignoring the chill in the air. She straddled his hips, working up her nerve by opening the buttons of his shirt, sliding her fingers through the hair there. He grunted, then again when she moved her sex closer to his, taking his cock in her hand and guiding it to the slickness of her body, rubbing it in the spot he'd caressed last night.

"What are you doing?" he growled, his hands whipping out to close around her wrists.

She snapped her gaze to his. She hadn't heard his breathing change, hadn't known he'd wake so easily. He scowled, his narrowed eyes on her bare breasts. Her nipples tightened in reaction, and his eyes darkened.

"I want to feel you inside me."

He huffed. "We can't. Not here."

"I want to feel you, Marcus." She dragged the head of his cock through the wet petals of her pussy. "Please let me take you."

He groaned and sat up. "Women don't take men."

She tightened her grip on his cock despite his hand still on her wrist. Finally he broke her grip, but instead of setting her aside, as she expected him to do, he cupped her breasts in his hands, bending his head to them, his lips and tongue rough on the sensitive flesh, his beard scratchy but so masculine. The tug of his mouth on her nipples seemed to connect her whole body to pleasure, and she jerked as he suckled her, his tongue flicking over the pebbled flesh and making her entire body wind up. She pressed her breasts closer to his mouth as her moisture pooled on his thighs. She bumped her hips forward, aching for the same release he'd given her last night, her pussy throbbing, needing to be filled.

He released her breasts and cupped her ass, bringing her forward, looking into her eyes as he slid into her heat, so slowly, stretching her. She held her breath as the sensations spiraled through her: the incredible pleasure of being stretched, the rasp of the hair of his groin against her tender nub, the security of his big body against hers.

Impatient, she moved her hips against his, taking him deeper. When he gasped, she did it again, taking him deeper still, until they were pressed completely together, the tip of his cock seated against her very center, their heartbeats in sync.

Her body contracted around him then relaxed, accommodating his girth and length, bringing him deeper. After taking him into her mouth last night, she'd wondered how he would fit inside but he did, just perfectly.

She began to move over him, her body aching for release as his cock rubbed inside her, her thighs burning as she pumped her hips against his. He strained beneath her, pressing up as if unwilling to leave her body, and together they struggled to find a rhythm.

Frustration tore at her when he pushed her off him so she straddled his thighs again and his erection rose between them.

"Get on your knees," he ordered.

After a moment's hesitation, she did, the roughness of his voice sending a shiver through her that settled in her nipples and pussy. She presented her ass to him. He glided his rough fingers over the smooth flesh before sliding against her cunt, spreading her folds. She angled her head to see him looking at her sex. He caught her gaze, gave her a slanted smile and positioned his cock against her entrance. Slowly, he slid into her from behind, this angle easier, his shaft deeper, the pleasure different, his cock seeming to press on the pleasure nub from the inside.

He pumped slowly into her wetness, pressing fully against her before withdrawing almost completely, the feeling exquisite as he dragged out her pleasure, and his. His rhythm quickened, his breathing changed, and he gripped her hips, plunging into her again and again, the friction exquisite, but still not enough. She cupped her own breasts, and liked that sensation, before she reached between her legs.

He made a choked sound when she touched the place they joined, when she pressed her fingers there to feel him moving in and out of her, his rhythm bordering on frantic. And then she touched her own nub, swollen and hot. Oh, it felt so different, so full with him inside her, stretching her.

His fingers dug into her hips as he plowed into her, each thrust pushing her against her own hand, until she hovered on the edge of climax.

Then he pushed her over, every fiber of her body whipping apart as if a cyclone hit, sending her flying in a breathtaking spiral. She hung suspended for a moment, as if she was above their joined bodies, looking down, before she descended to join herself again. Her channel clamping down on him, making him groan. He pulled free and she felt his hot seed stripe her bottom before she tumbled forward, spent, and he fell after her.

Lord, he was big and heavy and sweating, his breath blowing hot against her back before he finally rolled off of her and faced the sky, one hand thrown over his face.

"I'm sorry."

She rose on her elbows to look at him. "Why?"

He squinted at her in the early morning light. "I treated you like a whore."

"I doubt whores have such a good time."

He made a sound of disgust and rolled from the bedroll, reaching for his clothes. "You're under my protection."

"And I woke you with sin in mind." She let her gaze slide down his body and he caught his breath. "Make no mistake that this was my choice, Marshal. One I'd make again."

* * *

THE ENDLESS RIDING and Marcus's silence gave Abigail nothing to do but think about last night. Making love with Marcus had been almost everything she'd imagined. His body aroused her, his mouth, even the way he looked at her.

At least now she knew how to find her own pleasure. Wouldn't that shock Marcus, to know another girl had shown her how to bring herself to climax?

"Something funny?" he asked.

She jolted and turned to see him watching her. "Why?"

"You're smiling."

She drew in a breath, and held it. "Thinking about last night. How I shocked you."

Oh, she did enjoy seeing the color rise on his cheeks. He huffed out a breath and stared at the back of his horse's neck.

"I have to say, I've never had that happen before, a woman putting her mouth on me." He glanced over at her. "How did you know about that?"

"I live at a home for wayward girls. We are not called that

because we are innocent. One of the girls told me how to do it, to satisfy a man without getting with child. She taught me other things, too," she added, watching his face closely. She was playing with fire, but she liked it. Maybe she was more of her mother's daughter than she'd expected.

"Like what?" he asked, his voice tight.

"She's the one that showed me a woman can have pleasure, too. She showed me just where to touch. Sometimes, she'd touch me, sometimes I'd touch her."

His eyes went a little wild, and his blush deepened. "Mrs. McBride knew?"

"Of course not, but with as many girls as were in the house, we had to share a bed. Some nights we'd get naked and one of us would lay on top of the other, and we'd rub our pussies together until we both came. One night, she did to me what I did to you."

He made a choked sound.

"She put her mouth on me, used her tongue and fingers. I've never known anything like it."

"Did you—do the same to her?" he managed.

"Oh yes. But only once."

"You didn't—like it?"

"I liked it fine. But something was missing."

He reined in his horse and snagged her leads as well. She looked up in surprise just as he slammed his mouth down on hers, hooking his arm around her waist and dragging her out of her saddle and onto his.

Her delighted laugh echoed off the mountain as he wriggled his fingers down the front of her denims, finding her swollen nub effortlessly. She dropped her head back against his shoulder and lifted her hips to his touch. She hadn't thought talking about her experiences with Judith would arouse her, but his fingers moved against her slick folds, into her wet channel. More than anything, she wanted to feel his cock inside her, but there was nothing around but muddy ground, not even a place to put a bedroll.

He thrust two fingers inside her, pumping them shallowly as he cupped her breast in his other hand, pinching her nipple through her shirt. She thought about his pleasure for only a moment before she pressed against his hand, letting the roughness of his fingers inside her make her mindless, carry her over in a pulsing climax that had her pussy squeezing his hand.

When she relaxed against him, he removed his hand and rested it on his own thigh. After her own breathing slowed, she felt his breath still coming hot and fast against her throat.

"Let me," she whispered, and motioned to dismount.

He unwrapped his arms from around her and she slid to the ground, only to hold her hand up to him again. Frowning, he reached down for her, but this time she swung up behind the saddle, on his bedroll. She was higher than he was, which amused her as she shifted closer and reached for the opening of his denims, where his cock strained.

He helped her unfasten his pants and free himself so she could wrap her hand around his hot flesh. She pressed close against his back, curling her legs around him as she began to stroke from base to tip in the same rhythm she'd used with her mouth last night. He pulsed beneath her palm, and his breath hitched as she deviated from her rhythm to run exploring fingertips over him, learning the terrain of him. He reached down to close her hand around him, and guided her back to the rhythm he liked.

She allowed the horse's pace to help her, tightening her grip when he sucked in a breath through his teeth. His whole body gathered when she increased her speed, her arm growing tired but wanting to do this for him.

And then he spilled over her hand, a low groan reverberating from him as he pushed up into her grasp, his hips pumping into her hand for a moment before he relaxed and took her hand from around him, wiping it on his own thigh.

Without a word, he stopped the horse and she slid down and went to mount her own horse while he tidied himself. Before he urged the horse forward, he gripped her reins and leaned close.

"Tonight, I'm going to have you properly."

Marcus drew up his mount, his pulse thudding in his throat as he looked down at the Indian war party below. About ten braves sat on painted ponies, wearing buckskins and carrying rifles. He and Abigail couldn't outrun them, and even if they could, he didn't know this area well enough to know where they could run, and how far away a safe escape would be. He edged his horse between Abigail and the group below, who stayed still, watching them.

"Do you think you can get back to town on your own?" he asked, unbuckling his rifle from his bedroll.

"What are you going to do?" Her voice shook with nerves, and her horse shifted restlessly.

"Whatever I need to do," he replied grimly, balancing the rifle in his hand.

"If you shoot first, they're certain to shoot back.

"I understand that." Did she think he'd never been in this situation before?

"Perhaps we can just tell them why we're here, who we're looking for."

Negotiate? She had to be out of her head. "Isn't Joseph an Indian? Won't they try to protect him?"

"I don't know, but I know if you start shooting, they'll kill us both—or worse. Isn't it worth a try?"

He looked at her a long moment, considering, before nudging his horse down the hill toward the band. "Stay behind me."

He didn't like this, didn't like this at all. They'd have to run their horses back up the hill to retreat, and these horses weren't the best mounts to begin with, but they'd been all the stable had to sell. At least if they'd remained on top of the ridge, they could have kept the hill between them and the Indians for a while.

The Indians remained still, though a few of the horses shifted as the newcomers approached. Marcus kept his gun balanced on his lap, knowing it would take precious seconds to lift and fire. No, he didn't like this plan.

So why was he going along with it?

Because their chances of survival were about even if they'd tried to run. Abigail was right about that.

"Speak English?" he asked, relieved that the Indians didn't raise their own guns at their approach.

One of the men prodded his horse forward. "A little."

"We're looking for some outlaws who came through here. We don't want any problem with you, don't want to intrude on your territory. We just want to find them."

The man who spoke English looked from Marcus to Abigail, and his eyes widened. "Belle?"

Abigail brought her horse forward, color tinting her cheeks. "Her daughter."

The man nodded sharply then said something to the other Indians. "Come," he said in English, and turned his horse with the others, beckoning them to follow.

Abigail and Marcus exchanged a glance before following.

The hairs on the back of Marcus's neck were on high alert as the Indians surrounded them, but none made a threatening move, none of them so much as glanced at his gun. He wanted to bring Abigail close, wanted to hold her on his saddle, keep her safe, but if they had to bolt, it was better she was on her own horse. Still, he nudged his mount as close as possible to hers. He could reach out and touch her if he wanted, but for the time being, he kept his hand on his rifle and his senses on high alert.

He studied the Indians. Based on the territory, he figured they were Comanche, which made his skin prickle. Would they kill him and rape Abigail? Why hadn't they killed him yet?

And how did they know Sweetheart Belle?

They rode all day in silence, reaching a camp of teepees as the sun was slipping below the mountains. At first Marcus thought it was a war camp, just for the braves, but women and children moved among the tents. He hadn't thought the tribe was this far south, but perhaps they'd migrated for winter.

He was uncertain if the presence of women and children boded better for his and Abigail's fate.

The warriors pulled up and dismounted, and the one who had recognized Belle in Abigail's face stepped up beside her horse and reached for her. She hesitated only a moment before allowing him to help her off her horse. She clung to the man a moment, her legs probably sore from the hours in the saddle without a break, before she released him and turned to Marcus.

"My husband," she said, and then said something in Comanche.

The woman was full of surprises.

The men turned to him, their expressions flat, but he got the feeling they were assessing him. Would her words save him, or doom him?

The man who still stood too close to Abigail nodded finally, and signaled for Marcus to dismount. Marcus did, rifle in hand, only to have the weapon snatched from him by one of the other braves.

Damn, that was his favorite gun.

He followed the brave who led Abigail to a nearby tent. He couldn't be lucky enough to find Joseph, Abe and Nate here, could he? No, he didn't think so. But maybe the Indians knew where he could look.

If they let him walk out of here.

He stepped into the teepee in time to see an old Indian rise and embrace Abigail. The smell of smoke and fat blended together to choke him in the close space, but at least it was warm.

The old man stepped back to look at Abigail. "I have not seen you since you were a child. You have your mother's strength."

Even in the dim light from the small fire, Marcus could see her blush. He didn't know the reason—was she ashamed of her mother, or proud? She didn't talk much about the woman.

"We're looking for my brother," she told him. "It's been too long since I've seen him."

The old Indian turned shrewd eyes to Marcus. "I think that is not the only reason you are seeking him."

"I want to keep him out of trouble," she admitted. "He's heading down a dangerous path."

The old Indian nodded. "I have not seen him or your father in many years."

"Joseph is not my father," she said.

The old Indian studied her a moment. "No, he is not. Your mother never told you his name."

Abigail shook her head and Marcus could see her body tense. Did the Indian know who her father was? Would he tell her? Did she want to know?

Instead, he stepped back and motioned to the brave who had brought her. "Feed them."

"He is law," the brave said with a gesture to Marcus.

Marcus jolted at that. He'd taken care not to wear his badge, and the men had not searched him.

"I know," the old man said. "But he will not do anything to put her in jeopardy."

How did the old man know that, too?

Marcus was still puzzling when Abigail slipped her hand into his and led the way out of the teepee. Marcus was aware of the close attention of the other men as they waited for the brave to follow and do the old man's bidding.

"Do you know him?" he asked Abigail, bending his head to hers.

"I remember coming to an Indian camp much like this as a girl, and staying awhile. I told you we were nomadic when I was young. But no, I don't remember."

Sweetheart Belle must have had endless depths of courage to stay in a Comanche camp with her daughter. He wondered, looking at Abigail's dark hair, if her father was an Indian.

He had to shift his thoughts as they walked into the center of camp, drawing the attention of the women and children, many of whom held resentment in their eyes. Did they, also, know he was a lawman?

The brave who led them spoke to a woman, gesturing to the kettle over the fire. The woman frowned then ladled out two helpings in earthenware bowls. The smell turned Marcus's stomach, but he tasted it anyway, keeping his gaze locked with the woman's as he battled the stinking stew down his throat. Her lips thinned, but her eyes no longer held the same anger.

Marcus chanced a glance at Abigail to see her doing the same, her expression serene as if the foul taste didn't bother her, as if the grease didn't coat her mouth, holding the flavor captive. Maybe it didn't. But it was warm, and it filled his empty stomach.

Abigail handed the bowl back, nodding her thanks. Marcus forced the last of the stew down, trying not to chew, and did the same. Damn, what he wouldn't give for a hit of his whiskey right now, to burn the taste out of his mouth and throat.

The brave said something to the women, two of whom stepped forward and took Abigail by the arms silently. Abigail stiffened as they tried to turn her away, but the brave bent to whisper something to her and she stopped resisting. Marcus took a step to follow, but three braves stepped into his path as she disappeared around one of the teepees.

Marcus wanted to fight his way to her, but he was unarmed, and she hadn't seemed alarmed by whatever the brave had told her. Still, he hated her out of his sight and jostled to try to see her.

"Where are you taking her?" he demanded, but no one replied. Instead, the braves turned him around. One shoved his bedroll at him, and another carried Abigail's satchel. They guided Marcus to the edge of camp. The first brave motioned him into a teepee.

It looked much like the last teepee they'd been in, with buffalo hides against the edge, though this one was smaller and had no fire.

"You wait here," the brave told Marcus.

"I need to see to our horses," Marcus said.

"They will be seen to." The brave started to duck out of the tent.

"Will Abigail stay here with me?"

"She will come shortly."

"Will we be free to go in the morning?" Marcus asked.

"That is not up to me," the brave replied, and disappeared.

Marcus paced the small area before leaning out the flap of the tent to see three braves sitting outside. They turned to look at him, not in a threatening way, but in a way that made him know he wasn't to leave. He let the flap fall and crossed to sit on the buffalo hides. He reached for his bottle of whiskey in his bedroll, but stopped short of opening it. He wanted to be alert in case Abigail needed him.

He wasn't sure how long he waited before the flap opened and Abigail walked in. She was dressed like one of the squaws, her hair down and straight over the pale buckskin dress that flowed over the curves of her breasts and hips and revealed her calves. She looked beautiful.

He cleared his throat. "Going to be hard to ride in that."

"I think they'll give me back my clothes in the morning." She sat beside him on the hides. "They wanted me clean for you."

Only then did Marcus see her shaking.

"Are we prisoners?" she asked.

"I don't know. I imagine we'll find out in the morning when we try to leave." He hoped the Indians didn't eat their horses, because he was pretty sure that was what kind of meat had been in the stew, and it hadn't been fresh. He didn't want to mention it to Abigail and alarm her.

He reached into his pack and pulled out a bottle of whiskey. He twisted off the cap and offered it to her first. She took a healthy swig, gave a little gasp at the burn and passed it back. He grinned and took a good swig, grateful for the searing of his mouth and throat to remove the taste of the horse stew.

"Why did you tell them I was your husband?"

"Because I didn't want them to give me to one of their soldiers."

"What if they'd killed me and done that anyway?" Which they might still do, so he had to be alert.

"I would have fought," she said with a shrug, reaching for his bottle again.

"Go easy, that's the last bottle I have."

She drank anyway, her nostrils flaring, and handed it back. "They may be listening, wondering if we truly are husband and wife."

The last thing Marcus wanted was to be caught naked by the Indians. "I think they might understand if we forgo the marital act after being in the saddle all day, while being held captive by Comanches."

"I'm not sure they will, and I'm not willing to be taken away from you and given to a brave." She began unlacing her dress at her shoulder. "Do you think you can make the sacrifice?"

Maybe it was the whiskey making him reckless, but he

grinned again when she peeled down the dress and bared her breasts to him. Damn, she was bold. He never thought a woman like her existed.

Never thought a woman like that would excite him.

"I think I might be able to manage it."

He dragged her onto his lap and latched his mouth over one hard brown nipple, rubbing his tongue against the underside, suckling lightly as he traced his fingertips over the curve of her other breast. She gasped her approval and tossed her head back, the move pushing her breasts toward him. He glided her hands down her sides to the dress that pooled on her waist, pushing his hips into hers.

She tugged her dress up, baring herself to him. He dragged his hands up her smooth thighs to her pretty pussy, the scent of her arousal filling the teepee. He stroked a fingertip over her soft petals, so slick and wet, and pushed two fingers into her, just a little, enough to make her groan. He pumped gently until she pushed back, taking his fingers deeper, her fingers digging into his shoulders. He rubbed his thumb back and forth over the nub at the top of her pussy until her breath came in hot little pants.

He removed his touch to open his britches then put his hands on her waist to push her to her feet. He rose to his knees, pushing her dress up and over her head.

"Beautiful," he whispered, his gaze traveling from her uptipped breasts over her slender waist to the curve of her hips and the alluring thatch of curls at the apex of her thighs. He ruffled his fingers through them, parting her nether lips to gaze at the pink flesh a moment, before he curved his arms around her back and lowered her to the hides. Pulse drumming in his ears, echoing in his cock, he stripped off his shirt and pants before lowering himself over her.

This was the first time he'd been skin to skin with a woman, his legs rasping along hers, her breasts against the hair of his chest, his cock nestled into the cradle of her thighs, aching to enter her. Her gaze locked with his, she curved her hand around the back of his neck and opened her legs to him. He slid against her heat, over the slickness of her.

He shifted and slid into her. She squeezed around him, and he stilled, savoring the sensation just a moment before pushing deeper, until his body was flush with hers. She arched her back and pushed against him, her legs spread wide, the insides of her thighs soft against his hips.

He moved gently inside her, with a slow roll of his hips when he wanted to pound into her, but she deserved better, deserved the pleasure he could give her.

He lowered his mouth to hers, trying not to think of the stories she'd told him about her time with Nate Holland, trying not to think about the Indians outside listening. Instead, he focused on her scent, on the feeling of her hair against his skin, her nipples against his chest, the way she moved her hands over his chest and back. Her tongue swept into his mouth, mimicking the movement of his cock inside her.

He cupped her breast, rubbing his thumb over her nipple, before he reached between them to stroke her petals.

The moment he touched her, she clamped around him like a vice, pussy and legs, holding him to her, not allowing him to move, only bumping her hips against his touch in an erratic rhythm that set him on the very edge of control.

Unable to stop himself, he pulled out of her, causing her to cry out. He slid down her body, cupping her hips in his hands and leaned toward her pussy. He'd never done this, never wanted to do it, but since she'd taken him into her mouth, he'd thought of nothing else. He kissed her lightly, felt the throb of her nub against his lips, and burrowed deeper, his tongue flicking out to stroke her, and her whole body tightened beneath his hands.

She tasted different than he expected, sweeter, and his tongue grew bolder, licking and caressing. He dipped his fingers into her channel, stretching her, feeling her open wider.

And then she softened under his tongue, her body undulating in pleasure, her juices coating his fingers. When her shuddering stopped, he lifted his head and rose over her again, plunging into her still-pulsing body, stroking hard and deep until his thighs burned, until his balls tightened, and he came, emptying into her as she curved her arms around him and held him to her.

* * *

HE WOKE BESIDE HER, looking at the fine bones of her face as the morning light filtered through the animal hide of the teepee. She was still naked, though nestled against him for warmth. He loved looking at her, the smoothness of her skin, the dips and curves of her body. He'd never known a woman like her.

Just when he was reaching for her, the flap was pushed aside and two braves strode in. Marcus rose to his knees, ready to defend Abigail, who woke with a start, but the braves grabbed him instead, one on each arm, and hauled him, naked, out of the teepee and into the early morning light, where they pushed him to his knees.

He looked up, shaking his hair from his face, to see several braves in a circle as the sun rose over the mountain. He was barely aware of Abigail rushing out of the teepee, tying her dress at the shoulders, before he saw the giant knife swipe toward him.

bigail's scream echoed through the camp as the tip of the blade sliced through the muscle of his chest. He danced back, trying to take in his surroundings, to see what other threat approached, to see what he could use as a weapon to defend himself. He swooped to grab a branch from the fire, wishing this part of the New Mexico Territory had bigger trees with heftier branches. Still, he swung with all his strength, bringing it against the brave's wrist. The knife went flying and Marcus scrambled after it.

He was stopped short by a hand in his hair, yanking him back and upright onto his knees. He met Abigail's terrified gaze as another blade sliced across his back. He dropped the branch to the dirt. Jesus, were they going to scalp him? Right in front of Abigail?

She raced toward him, only to be caught up by another brave, who laughed when she kicked and twisted in his arms. She screamed Marcus's name, a sound that echoed in his head as the blade bit again. He was vaguely aware of the brave dropping her, bending over. She scrambled on all fours across the dirt toward him, holding her hand up as a knife sliced down.

She cried out as blood blossomed across her palm then pressed herself against him like a shield. The pressure on his scalp eased, and he sensed some of the braves backing off.

But another grabbed her, pulled her from him and tossed her in the dirt. The man dropped over her, pinning her to the ground. With a roar, Marcus lunged forward. He grabbed the man by the shoulder and flipped him off of Abigail. His enemy dropped to a crouch, waving his blade at Marcus, who was unarmed again.

He was aware of Abigail rolling out of the way. All he wanted was her safe. But then she came back with a rock from the fire and slammed it against the brave's head. He went down. The jeering crowd silenced when he went still, blood seeping into the dirt around him.

Marcus took advantage, snatched up the fallen knife and launched himself at Abigail, grabbing her arm and dragging her toward the tent and their belongings. They'd have to get what they could, as fast as they could, because he'd be damned if he was riding bareback while buck-naked.

They'd have to steal horses, and didn't have time for saddles. Hell, if he had pants on, he wouldn't waste time going into the teepee. From the corner of his eye, he saw Abigail shoving her things and some of his into that damned satchel. For once the thing was coming in handy, faster to pack than his bedroll. He dragged on his pants, grabbed his boots, and used the knife to cut an escape into the back of the teepee.

He wished to hell he knew where they put his gun, because they were in big trouble without weapons, but already he heard the sound of pursuit. He took her satchel and they ran out the back of the teepee.

Both of them were barefoot as they raced down the hill to where he thought the horses might be corralled. Damn, Abigail was going to have a hard time riding bareback in that dress, but he couldn't let them take her. He had a good idea of what they'd do to her, and he couldn't let that happen.

Some braves stood near the fenced area where the horses were kept, and they looked up in surprise when Abigail and Marcus barreled toward them. Marcus vaulted the rough wood fence of the corral and grabbed a horse by the mane, reaching to help Abigail over. Even barefoot, she did pretty well on her own.

Behind them, their pursuers crested the rise and poured down the hill toward them, shouting. He thought about pulling her up on the horse with him, but she selected her own horse and used the fence to boost herself onto the animal's back. Marcus wheeled his mount toward the gate of the corral, where the braves gathered to stop them. Marcus crouched on the horse's back, urging him forward, forcing the braves to break for cover or be run down. Abigail's squeal made him turn. One of the braves caught her ankle and was pulling her from the horse. Marcus pivoted and charged his animal toward the man, who glared, challenging, not releasing Abigail until Marcus's horse was almost up on him. The brave fell backward and Abigail's horse bolted forward.

"Stay close!" Marcus shouted, and guided his horse up the hill behind the camp, needing to put the landform between them and their enemies, needing to do it while the horses were fresh.

Above the shouts of the Indians, he heard the thunder of her horse's hooves behind him. He wished he knew this area better, wished he knew someplace he could keep her safe. He doubted there were any towns nearby, not with such a large Comanche settlement here. A fort, maybe, but where? How long could they ride at this speed without being overtaken? They were unarmed. What chance did they have?

A better chance than if they'd stayed in camp. He had to believe that as he bent low over his mount, holding onto its mane. He chanced a glance at Abigail to see her doing the same, her strong thighs gripping the horse's withers, her expression determined. There was something to be said about her growing up wild.

He turned his attention to their escape, feeling his lungs expand finally when they were over the hill and had the expanse of land below them. He scanned for only a moment before nudging his horse toward what looked like a river, a line of trees snaking across the plains. If it was a river, they'd be likely to find a settlement eventually. And even if it wasn't, the trees would offer some cover.

He eased back to keep his horse between their pursuers and Abigail, knowing at the same time that if he was killed, he couldn't protect her. Hell, without a weapon, he couldn't protect her.

The horses rode flat-out beneath them, as alarmed by the noise of their pursuers as Marcus and Abigail. The trees loomed distant, and the cold wind stung Marcus's bare skin. Damn, if they got away, he didn't think they had any bedding to keep them warm. And what had become of Abigail's denims and shirts? She couldn't go far dressed in a buckskin dress.

The sound of pounding hooves made him glance over his shoulder. The Indians had jumped on their horses to pursue. Marcus hoped the horse beneath him had stamina, because otherwise...

Abigail's sob of relief carried back to him as they reached the trees. She ducked low over the horse's back to avoid the branches. Though he copied her maneuver, the branches scratched his naked back and arms.

That was nothing compared to what the Indians would do if they caught up.

The obstacles of the trees slowed them, and would slow their pursuers as well. But the Indians had the advantage of knowing the land, knowing what lay beyond.

Their shouts rang through the woods. He chanced a glance

and saw they were getting closer, waving their guns. He hoped they were conserving bullets.

Beneath him, his horse was flagging. Sweat slicked the brown coat and flecked off with each step. He looked at Abigail and saw her kicking her heels into her horse's side but wasn't getting the same speed.

They had to find someplace to hide, and soon.

The horses pounded to the top of a ridge, and Marcus looked down at the river below.

He looked over at Abigail. She'd said she could swim, but was it worth the risk to jump into the water and let the current carry them?

He looked up and down the bank. One direction had a hill that would slow the horses further, the other had thick trees. They might be able to hide in the trees, but for how long?

Beneath him, his horse's sides heaved. The mount wouldn't be good for much longer. He measured the risks.

"Abigail."

Her face pale, she swallowed and nodded.

He slid off the horse, holding onto her satchel, with the only supplies they owned, and reached for her hand. He hoped the river was deep enough—the current certainly looked fast enough. No telling where they'd end up, if they survived the jump.

Or if they'd freeze to death.

Better than being cut to pieces.

She tightened her fingers around his and took the first step as a gunshot rang out behind them. She turned her head to look at him as they leapt, then closed her eyes and screamed on the way down.

The cold water shocked the breath from him, and he had a moment to assess the irony that only yesterday he'd endeavored to stay out of the water before he went under.

His lungs screamed as the current tumbled him so that he

didn't know which was the surface and which was the bottom. He had to find the surface, had to find Abigail.

Something snagged his hair, jerking at him, tearing at his scalp. He reached up to dislodge whatever it was holding onto him only to encounter a small hand.

Abigail.

And she seemed to be steady in the water. He grabbed her wrist and held on, loosening the strain on his scalp. She gave another tug and he broke the surface, gulping in a deep lungful of air as the water swirled around him. He wrapped his arm around her waist and looked into her face, the water dripping from her lashes, her lips parted on shallow pants.

He looked past her to see she was holding onto a fallen tree. He released her to grab onto a thicker branch, closer to the bank, and fought to bring her with him.

Before he could find his footing, the branch snapped, and the two of them tumbled back into the water.

This time, he didn't let go of her arm, keeping contact with her even as the rocks below struck his legs.

He had no idea how far they were swept before the current slowed and he was able to pull them toward the bank. With the last of his strength, he dragged Abigail into the mud and collapsed beside her, listening to her panting in rhythm with his. When he looked at her, though, her skin was waxy with the cold. They needed to get moving, anything to warm up.

Without waiting for her to catch her breath, he pulled her to her feet and dropped the satchel on the ground.

"Everything's bound to be wet, but at least get your boots on," he instructed, reaching inside for his own.

"I can't believe you held onto it," she chattered, taking the drenched socks he handed her.

"It's got everything we own." Once his boots were on, he rummaged for a shirt, handed her one to put on over the buckskin dress, and dragged one on himself. Damn, the wet fabric was almost worse than the wind on his skin. He buttoned up and straightened, looking north, then south.

"Which way?" she asked, wrapping her arms around herself.

"There's probably a town or a fort to the north," he said, picking up the satchel. "But we just came that way and would have to pass the Indian camp to get to civilization. I say we go south. There's bound to be a town along the river at some point."

How many days it would take them to get to it was another question. And each step in wet socks rubbing against wet boots would be torture. That, and looking at Abigail's chilled legs. He hoped the wind dried their skin soon, and that the sun would rise over the mountains and warm them.

He kept an eye on her as they walked. They hadn't eaten since last night's stew, and they had no food. Even if they saw wildlife, he had no way to kill it. She was quiet, and her steps a little stiff. He wouldn't ask, but he wondered if she wished she was back at the home for wayward girls, where she'd be warm, dry and fed.

Hell, he wished *he* was back there now.

Finally, the sun did crest over the mountains, but its watery light gave little warmth. The only sound was their heavy footfalls and breathing that grew labored the longer they went on.

"Do you want to rest?" he asked at last.

She only shook her head, her gaze in front of her.

"Abigail. If you need to rest, it doesn't mean you're weak."

"No point in resting if I can keep going and we can get someplace safe."

He looked over his shoulder. "I don't think they'll come after us."

"No? Why wouldn't they? They seemed intent on seeing you dead."

"If they were pursuing us, they would have caught up by now," he pointed out. "They have horses."

"Our horses," she muttered. "You don't think they'll eat them or anything, do you?"

"They'll ride them," he said, wishing he could be sure.

She trudged along, tying her hair back from her face with another strand of hair. "So once we get to civilization, providing we don't end up in Mexico, what then? Are we still going after Joseph and Abe?"

"I have no choice. I can, however, send you back to the home, or anywhere you want to go."

She snapped her gaze in his direction. "You'd do that?"

He couldn't tell if her voice held hope or outrage. "I haven't done a good job of keeping you safe. I need to send you back before something else happens."

She didn't argue, but kept walking. An uneasiness rose in him. Why wasn't she arguing, and how exactly did he feel about that?

"Did you know my mother?" she asked.

"What?" Where had that come from?

"You came to tell me she was dead. Did you know her?"

"I met her once." He'd been a newly minted deputy and dazzled by the beautiful woman, even more impressed by her nerve, flirting with him when she knew he knew who she was.

"She was strong."

"I suppose you could say that, though she wasn't wise about using her strength. If she was, she'd still be here. She put herself at risk and left you and your little brother alone with an outlaw who did not have your best interest at heart."

"She did what she had to do. Women don't have a lot of choices, and she made a hard one. At least we didn't grow up in a brothel."

"You're defending her robbing banks and killing people?"

"No, I'm not. I'm just saying she made a hard choice when she didn't have much to choose from."

He frowned. "She was the one who ran wild and took the choices women usually have away from herself."

"As I've done? First I ran away with Nate, ruining my reputation, and now I've run off with you. My fate is sealed. I'll never be a proper lady."

He pressed his lips together, unaware that had been a trap. "You haven't run into banks demanding money and shooting people. Shooting lawmen."

Her breath caught. He'd been with the marshal who'd come to tell her that her mother was dead. Had he seen her that day? "You were there the day she died."

"I was. She didn't get into the bank that day. We knew she was coming and had cleared the area of innocent bystanders and surrounded the entrance of the bank."

"You saw her shoot someone."

"I did. She shot him in the head, Abigail. Just stood there, lifted her gun and fired, then kept walking."

She gave a shudder. "Did you know him?"

"I did. He was a young man whose wife was expecting their first child. In her grief, she lost the baby, too."

She stopped to face him, her chin quivering just a bit, her eyes bright with tears. "Did you kill my mother, Marcus?"

He took a deep breath. "I ran toward her, dodging behind a wagon when she fired in my direction, when Joseph approached, covering her back. He looked right into my eyes as he fired at me. That gave one of the posse the opening he needed to shoot your mother." He didn't want to look into her eyes anymore, but knew he must.

"Did she die right away?"

Blood had been everywhere on the boardwalk, the bullet having pierced her breast, just as Finney had said. Joseph had stared at her for a moment before he'd vaulted over her prone body and raced for the horses. Marcus remembered the gunshots ringing out after a moment of stillness, of disbelief. He'd been the first to reach Belle, expecting her to be dead, shocked when she'd blinked those beautiful blue eyes at him once, twice, before the life faded from her.

"Pretty close to right away. Only a few moments. Joseph, the man who claimed to have loved her, ran off and left her to die alone on the boardwalk."

Abigail turned to start walking again. She said nothing for a long time. "Did they string her up? I'd heard they strung her up and left her body for everyone to see."

He was glad she was no longer looking at him. "They did. I'm sorry, Abigail."

She shook her head. "I know what she did was wrong. I know it. But she was my mother and I loved her. She loved me. I just...wanted to know." After a moment, she added, "I'm glad you didn't kill her."

He didn't want to say he would have, had he been closer. "So am I."

* * *

THE SUN WENT behind the mountains early in the day, but their clothes were dry, for the most part, so the wind wasn't as chilly. Though the sky above was still bright, Marcus started looking for a place to sleep. The idea of sleeping in the wild unarmed did not appeal, but they didn't have many options. The idea of sleeping on the cold ground, even with Abigail in his arms—if she'd come to his arms, after what he'd told her about her mother's death—made him uneasy.

Maybe they could at least find a cave to shelter them from the wind. He was shaking from hunger. Maybe he could make a snare from some of their clothes, though he didn't know how they'd bait it.

Moot point since he couldn't find a safe place for them to stop. Maybe over the rise.

But before they reached the rise, he saw eight horsemen riding away from them. He grabbed Abigail and dragged her to her belly on the ground before he realized they weren't Indians or outlaws.

"Soldiers!" he said, and climbed to his feet, pulling her with him. He put his fingers to his lips and whistled sharply, but the soldiers kept riding. He wet his lips and whistled again, long and shrill, and one of the soldiers looked back. Marcus waved his arms as he headed down the hill, dragging Abigail with him.

Still the soldiers didn't stop, and Marcus whistled again.

Finally, three of the soldiers turned their horses, circled them to confer before two broke away from the group and rode toward them. Marcus drew up and waited, quivering with cold and hunger, and awareness of the possibility that the soldiers would treat them as hostile. He brought Abigail against his side and waited as the horses thundered toward them.

As they approached, Marcus saw their uniforms were ill-kept and faded, and their beards were poorly groomed. Were they close to a fort, or had they been on their own for a while?

"Who are you?" the first soldier barked.

From his insignia, Marcus knew he was a sergeant, higher ranking than the others who accompanied him. "I'm Marshal Marcus Grey, and this is my wife, Abigail."

One of the soldiers looked at Abigail, taking in her buckskin dress. "Not your squaw?"

Marcus stiffened. "We escaped from a camp of Indians just north of here along the river. Comanche."

"You escaped?" the soldier scoffed. "How?"

"We jumped into the river. All we have is what we're carrying. We haven't eaten all day. Do you have any food?"

The soldier who remained silent reached into his bag and pulled out some pemmican. He handed it to Marcus, who passed it to Abigail. She turned big eyes to him, tore the tough meat in half and handed him the larger piece. He protested, but she frowned and offered it again. His stomach pitched, and he tore his teeth into it.

The flavor made his mouth water, and his stomach rolled. Food, but not enough. He chewed and watched the sergeant.

"Is your camp far?" he asked.

"We have a fort a few miles to the south."

"Can you take us?"

The soldiers eyed Abigail and her bare legs. "Can she ride?"

"I can," she said, tilting her chin up.

The quiet soldier reached his hand down to her, and the sergeant held his hand to Marcus. Once mounted behind the smaller man, Marcus looked over to Abigail, whose head dropped with relief against the soldier's shoulder.

* * *

THE FORT WAS SMALLER than Abigail expected, hardly bigger than the George P. Williamson Home for Wayward Girls. She wondered how many soldiers were stationed here, and how many women. The way they looked at her, in her buckskin dress that bared most of her legs as she rode astride behind the soldier, she had a feeling there were not many women in residence.

Once they were safe inside the walls, Marcus hopped from the back of the horse he was riding and walked over to reach for her. She slid gratefully into his arms and hung on for a long moment, glad that he seemed to want to hold onto her as well.

The leader, Captain Sanders, gestured to a cook pot close to the edge of camp. Marcus almost stumbled in his haste to get to it, and once they had the warm bowls of stew in their hands—though to be honest, it wasn't any more flavorful than the stew in the Indian camp—Marcus turned to the captain.

"Can we get my wife some warm clothes? We lost about everything we had when we fled from the Indian camp."

The captain inspected her long enough to make her step behind Marcus.

"We don't have any women in camp," he replied.

"I'll wear trousers," she said. "It makes it easier to ride astride."

The older man's lips turned down in disapproval.

"She needs something warm to wear," Marcus pressed, curving his arm around her waist and pulling her to his side.

The captain blew out a breath. "I'll see what I can do."

Shortly, they were taken to a rough-walled room with a narrow bed, a window and a chamber pot. Abigail crossed the room to cover the window with a blanket from the bed, and turned toward the bed. Marcus would not be able to fit in that with her.

"I'll sleep in the barracks," he told her, reading her thoughts. "You have the room to yourself."

She didn't like that idea, being alone in a strange place, surrounded by all the men who'd looked at her so openly. "Wouldn't it be just as comfortable to sleep in here on the floor?"

He looked into her eyes for a moment, considering. "I suppose." He turned to the captain. "Is there extra bedding?"

The captain excused himself to see to it as Abigail put one sore foot in front of the other and collapsed on the bed. She shivered so violently that Marcus had to pull the blankets over her. For a moment, he stretched out beside her, his warmth seeping through the blankets to her skin. She quivered even as he wrapped his arms around her and bent his head to hers.

At last, lethargy took over, and she sank into sleep.

When she woke, the camp was dark and the room was silent. She didn't hear Marcus's breathing. When she fumbled to find a lantern to light, she saw that he wasn't in the room. Her heart gave a panicked lurch. Where was he? Had he left her here alone?

She looked around the room, but no one had brought her clothes. She dug through her ruined satchel to find only blouses, no skirts. She didn't want to walk around this camp in her buckskin dress. But she couldn't go to sleep, not knowing where he was.

Raucous laughter carried across the courtyard, but she didn't know if Marcus was one of the voices—she'd never heard him laugh. She thought she'd heard drinking wasn't allowed in army forts, but perhaps this fort was so far from civilization, no one cared to follow the rules.

She wanted to investigate, but a woman alone—no. She was smarter than that. She crept to the window and peeked out past the blanket she'd hung for privacy. If she angled her head just right, she could see into the window of the common room, could see men in their unbuttoned army coats drinking deeply from tin mugs. When she'd been growing up, some scruffy looking men had frequented her home, and to her eyes, these men were no different, living on the outside of society, living in the wild. Their purposes might be different, but the feeling she got from them was the same.

The door to her room rattled and she spun around to face it, at the chair she'd wedged under the doorknob after Marcus had left.

"Abigail, it's me."

Marcus's voice was slurred but recognizable. She crossed the small room and pulled the chair free, and the door swung inward.

He swayed there for a moment, the scent of whiskey washing toward her on the breeze. She wondered for a moment if she should help him, but then he stepped inside, sure-footed, and cupped his hand behind her head. He angled his mouth over hers in a sweeping kiss that ran the length of her body and back up, curling her toes, weakening her knees, before pooling between her legs.

She lifted her tongue to meet his, savoring the taste of him, the warmth of his hard body as she pressed against him. His thumb brushed her cheek and he pressed his other hand to the small of her back, bringing her even closer. She wound her arms around his neck and twisted her fingers in his hair. He grunted and backed her toward the bed, then broke the kiss to eye the narrow cot. He sat on the cot, solidly in the middle, and drew her forward, so she straddled his lap, her buckskin dress riding up on her hips, baring her to the waist. He glided his hands up her thighs to close over her hips, bringing her forward. He lifted his face to kiss her, his fingers kneading her bottom as he lifted his hips to hers so the front of his breeches rubbed against her sex. She gasped into his mouth and held perfectly still, the muscles of her thighs quivering, and he lifted his hips again.

He held her on such an edge, she couldn't even kiss him, her mouth hovering above his, his breath hot on her lips as he lifted his hips again, this time not as high, only teasing her to move against him.

Heat washed over her in a wave, melting everything away, every fear, every doubt, leaving nothing but him and her.

She was vaguely aware of him freeing his cock from his britches and guiding it to her. She lifted to welcome him, gasping as her pulsing body accepted him.

"So hot," he said against her skin, twisting her hair away from her throat to touch his lips to it. "So wet. God, you have no idea how good you feel."

His words made her skin tingle. As if he knew it, he slid his hands over her skin under the buckskin dress, pushing it up her body and over her head. He cupped her breasts, circling his thumbs over her nipples, watching her face as he did.

She closed her eyes, unable to bear the intensity of his gaze, and gave herself over to the building sensation as he caressed her back to arousal.

"The most beautiful woman I've ever seen," he murmured.

He rubbed his lips against the line of her throat, his beard tickling, sending sparks through her blood until she thought fire would shoot from her fingertips. His fingers tightened on her bottom, showing her the rhythm he wanted, and he waited for her to match it, rolling against him, feeling him swell inside her. Her little bud, hard again, brushed the hair of his groin and pulsed with the need for completion. She rose on her knees for better leverage as she increased the speed of her thrusts. She slammed her mouth down on his, catching his ragged breathing into her lungs. Her fingertips dug into his shoulders, and she realized belatedly that while she was naked, he was not. The idea excited her even more and she rode him hard until he gave a choked gasp and gripped her hips, stilling her over him.

She felt his cock jerk inside of her, and then the warmth of his seed spill into her, but she wasn't done. She was close, and he wouldn't let her move.

"Marcus," she pleaded.

His eyes were glazed as he looked at her, but understanding dawned. He lifted her off him, his cock sliding free, and turned her to lie on the bed. Still dressed, still semi-hard, he knelt between her legs and teased the lips of her pussy apart. His rough fingers traced her slick opening, dipping inside, before he dragged them up through her petals to circle the throbbing little nub. She lifted her hips toward him, and he chuckled.

"Seems hardly fair you get to go twice, and me just once."

For a moment, she thought he'd pull away, just to keep things even between them. She might go out of her mind if he did that. But no, he stroked his finger up and down the length of the bundle of nerves, watching as he did so. She thought she probably should be embarrassed, the way he was looking at her, but no. No, the way he studied her heightened her arousal.

Then he blew a stream of breath against her hot skin and she exploded, bowing off the cot, a cry of pleasure tearing from her throat as her entire body throbbed and burned with the force of the climax.

He clamped his free hand over her mouth and chuckled as applause sounded from outside the window.

Despite the narrow cot, he stretched out beside her, bringing her close against the heat of his body, and drew a blanket over both of them. He was asleep before she'd even closed her eyes.

* * *

HE WOKE her from a deep sleep by shaking her shoulder, and she glanced toward the window, where weak light was penetrating the blanket she'd hung.

"What is it?"

"The stage is coming. I need to get you on it."

The stage. She pushed back the blankets and sat up, more relieved than she expected at the thought of returning to civilization.

"Where are we going?" she asked, wondering what she would wear. Certainly not her buckskin dress.

"You are going back to Padilla. I am going after Joseph."

He didn't meet her gaze as he said it, as he removed his belongings from her ruined satchel. She stared at his brisk movements, her entire body iced over, and not because of the temperature in the room.

"You're sending me away?" But she had no place to go. And after last night, when he made love to her so thoroughly? Was he saying good-bye?

"I'm making sure you're safe." He straightened and turned to her then, his gaze direct, the eyes that had looked at her with such heat last night now emotionless. "I didn't ask you to come on this trek, and I cannot guarantee your safety."

She pushed from the cot, aware she was naked but not caring. Her anger and hurt warmed her through and through, sending a red flush through her body.

"I never asked you to guarantee anything. I came with you to save my brother and that's what I intend to do."

His jaw clenched. "The soldiers will sell me one horse and one gun, and one set of clothing for you to wear back to civilization. Even if I wanted to, I couldn't take you with me."

Even if I wanted to. The words staggered her, but she couldn't let him see it. She should have known better, should have listened to the lessons the other girls at the home had taught her. Never allow yourself tender feelings for a man, because he will disappoint you every time.

She had too much pride to beg, though the thought of traveling alone, of having nothing when she got to her destination, nothing of her own but her boots and her satchel, made her knees watery.

He stepped forward and touched her bare arm, but she backed away, quicker than she would have liked. She didn't want him to see how upset she was.

"I'm sending you to one of my friends in the marshal service. He'll set you up, make sure you have something to live on."

Until when, she wanted to ask. Was Marcus intending to come for her, once his job was over?

No, she couldn't even allow herself that hope.

Perhaps she could get a job as a housekeeper, or a governess, anything to keep her out of the brothel.

Why had she been so impulsive? Why hadn't she looked to the future? Apparently, that was a trait she shared with her mother.

She wasn't going to argue with him. As much as she wanted to find her brother and set him straight, she knew her presence had been a stress on Marcus. It was more important that Marcus find her brother before he was killed than for her to go with him.

Perhaps she should have thought of that before, and Abe would be safe already.

"Abby. Are you okay?"

She snapped her head up. He'd never called her that before, and his tender tone could be her undoing.

"I'm fine," she said briskly. "I understand there isn't transportation for both of us, and I won't be a hardship to you any longer."

"Abigail."

His tone was resigned, and that he used her full name made

her sad. "If you'll just see about getting me proper clothes, please. I don't have anything to pack."

He took a step toward her, his brow furrowed, his mouth drawn down. He lifted a hand as if he wanted to touch her then lowered it to his side again and left.

* * *

SHE DIDN'T CRY until she was in the stagecoach, squeezed against the side by a middle-aged couple, Mr. And Mrs. Hemphill. Her legs were drawn up against the seat because of the lounging soldier across from her, who'd boarded the stage at the fort as well. He didn't disguise his contempt, his gaze traveling up and down her body, clothed in borrowed britches and shirts. While she was grateful to be out of the buckskin dress, she still felt exposed now that she was back with civilized folk. She mustered some of the strength she had discovered in the past two days and ignored him, and the disdainful woman beside her.

The fifth passenger was an older gentleman, Mr. Beedle, who had a kind smile but said not a word. Of course, once the stage was on the road, no one spoke—it was too difficult to carry on a conversation above the rattling of the wheels on the hard ground.

Thank goodness they hadn't encountered any mud from the rain of the past few days. The stage moved easily over the hard-packed roads.

Marcus had told her she would arrive in Padilla in a day, but it was a long day of travel. And she had nothing to occupy her thoughts but Marcus.

He had not kissed her good-bye. She hadn't expected him to, really, not in front of the soldiers, though they thought she was his wife. He'd handed her into the coach next to Mrs. Hemphill, then stepped back and closed the door. He hadn't said a word, just watched her silently as the coach pulled away.

She could still feel the roughness of his hand on hers, and if she closed her eyes, she could still see the pleasure on his face when she'd taken him.

She had to stop doing that to herself. She was certain she'd never see him again.

Mrs. Hemphill was attempting to read the Bible. The very thought made Abigail nauseous as the coach swayed side to side. So she turned again to the window and the passing landscape that never changed, endlessly brown and barren.

The stage stopped for luncheon on the side of the road. The soldier, Sergeant Lufkin, and she had simple fare packed by the fort. The Hemphills had a spread of food that made Abigail's stomach growl in envy. Mr. Beedle joined the married couple, but Abigail would be damned if she pretended to be someone she was not merely for a good meal.

So she sat alone in the shade of the stage and ate her sandwich. She would be glad her stomach wasn't so full once the stage started moving again. The motion made her stomach pitch. She wondered if that was what it was like to ride on a ship on the ocean.

"You've never been on a stage before," the soldier observed when everyone returned to their seats.

"And I hope never to be again." But at least she was warm and fed and not walking across the desert.

"Have you ever been on a train?" he asked. "Much smoother and faster. Once we get to Padilla, I'll get on the train and head east to Fort Worth. Where are you going?"

"I'll stay in Padilla with a friend of my husband's." Her tongue didn't trip over the words, though her mind did.

"Until he finds the outlaws."

"Yes."

"I never knew of a marshal taking his wife on such a journey."

"It was not intentional. We were traveling when he learned of this group of outlaws. He wanted to leave me in town from the beginning, but I insisted."

"Not many women would do something so foolish."

"No," she agreed, and looked out the window again, hoping to end the conversation. She was not good at lying, and didn't want to think about her "husband" anymore.

A bank of clouds was on the horizon, and she shivered, expecting more rain. Rain would slow their journey, and she just wanted it done with. She wanted to know her future instead of being held in this transition.

Unbidden, her thoughts turned to Marcus, traveling alone, moving faster, no doubt, but he would be miserable in the rain. Would he be able to find shelter? Would he be warm enough? She focused on the cloud and tried to imagine what he was doing at that moment.

The falling snowflakes caught her by surprise. She hadn't thought the air was cold enough, and again her thoughts went to Marcus. She was warm now, crammed in the stage with strangers, but he was out in the wind and the wet.

She was so busy watching the spinning flakes fall, she didn't hear the thunder of hooves over the sound of the stage until it was too late. Panic rolled through the stage as the woman beside her tried to hide herself and her husband, and the soldier and the older gentleman drew their weapons.

The stage rattled to a halt, and someone from the front shouted, "Abigail Vincent! Show yourself!"

CHAPTER 7

$\mathcal{M}$arcus was miserable. He huddled over his horse, his hat pulled low against the falling snow. At least he hadn't dragged Abigail along with him. She was safe and warm and had food, and when she arrived in Padilla, the sheriff would take care of her, take her home to his family until Marcus got to her.

Then what? He wasn't a man meant to have a family. His job certainly didn't allow for a family. He'd never be home.

Maybe he could find a way, if he knew Abigail was waiting for him. No other woman had ever made his thoughts wander down this path. She was tough and beautiful, strong and arousing. That she hadn't argued to come with him surprised him, but the way she'd avoided his eyes told him she was hurt by his decision.

Right now he was grateful for it.

He lifted his hat enough to look out over the landscape. It wasn't snowing enough to look for shelter, despite the horse beneath him twitching her withers in protest as the snowflakes melted against her.

He dragged his thoughts back to the case at hand. At least he had a lead. Captain Sanders had shown him a canyon on the map just northeast of here, and Abigail had said they'd once stayed in a hideout in a canyon. Captain Sanders had said yes, there was a building, but he'd never had reports of people in it from soldiers who'd been on patrol.

That was fine. If the outlaws were holed up there, not expecting trouble, the easier on him.

* * *

Abigail craned her head to look out the window of the stage. Her stomach sank as she saw long black hair streaming from beneath a black hat. Not the Comanches—they didn't know her name in any case.

It was Joseph.

Beyond him, she saw two other riders, out of the line of fire. Abe and Nate? Her heart kicked at the sight of her brother, who she barely recognized. He'd become a man in the years they'd been apart.

How had they found her? How had they known she was here?

"Abigail Vincent! Come with us, and we'll leave peacefully."

Well. Hadn't she been looking for them this past week? She should feel fortunate they found her. She reached for the handle of the door.

The soldier grabbed her hand. "What do you think you're doing?"

"Going with them. They promised no one would be hurt."

"Let her go," Mrs. Hemphill said nervously. "We don't want trouble."

"I'm supposed to protect her," the soldier said.

That gave Abigail another jolt. "Marcus sent you?"

The young man met her gaze. "He wanted you looked after."

She broke free of his hold and opened the door. "Tell him where I am. He'll want to know." She slid down from the stage, shivering a bit as the wind hit her skin, and folded her arms over her stomach as she looked up at her stepfather on the big bay.

"You finally decided to come for me?"

He grunted and turned his horse as Abe nudged his forward. Her brother gave her the smile she'd last seen on his face six years ago. Her eyes misted with tears as she moved toward him. Instead of dismounting and embracing, he held his hand to her and swung her onto the saddle behind him, then wheeled his horse and nudged it into a gallop, followed by Joseph and the third man. She held tight to her brother and pressed her face into the back of his coat.

Her brother. She'd found him.

She flinched at the sound of gunfire behind them, bracing herself for the impact of a bullet, but then the stage drove off, harnesses and wheels rattling.

Abigail didn't look back.

They rode hard through the cold air and the snow, so she huddled into Abe's slender back. She was surprised when Nate pulled alongside their horse and tossed a horse-scented blanket around her shoulders. The warmth seeped into her instantly, and she curled her hands into it to hold it around her, offering him a shaky smile of thanks that he returned with a flashy one of his own.

One she remembered could charm her into his bed. Her stomach clenched. She hadn't seen him since he'd been arrested and she'd been sent to the home for wayward girls. So much time had passed—what did she say to him now? What did she say to any of them?

He pulled ahead and led the way until they reached a canyon, then slowed as they entered the narrow passageway. None of the men had spoken to her since they left the stage.

And the question that niggled most—how had they found her?

They drew up their horses in front of a ramshackle cabin.

Joseph dismounted and strode to her, reaching to help her off the back of Abe's horse. He held onto her a moment, until she pushed free.

By then, Abe had dismounted and swept her into his arms.

Up in his arms. He was taller than her, and strong. She could feel how hard and strong he was beneath the thickness of his coat. She wrapped her arms around his shoulders and hugged him before drawing back to look at his face. Eyes like hers, like their mother's, but everything else was Joseph, the strong chin, the high cheekbones, the lean planes of his cheeks. He was a man now. She touched his cheek and stepped back.

If he got caught robbing banks or trains or stages, he'd be hung as a man, or shot in the commission of the crime without a thought.

Why had Joseph dragged him into this life?

"You look terrible, sister."

Probably because she hadn't slept well in almost a week. "I've been looking for you."

"We know," Joseph said, and inclined his head toward the cabin. "With a marshal."

"I came with him to keep Abe safe." She had a hard time making her point with her teeth chattering so she pulled the blanket tighter around her shoulders as she walked into the cabin.

The air inside was no warmer, and no surprise, with the chinks between the wooden planks letting the cold air in. The one window was on the far side of the cabin, the north side, so it let in very little light. Everyone's face was in shadow once the door closed behind them and she pivoted on Joseph.

"How can you do this to your own son, put his life in danger like this? Don't you see that he could be killed?"

"You think you can come back here in my house after you ran away, and tell me what to do?" Joseph countered, leaning forward, the line of his body a threat.

"I can when you're hurting my brother."

"Who you haven't cared to see in how many years?"

She seethed. "I haven't had the money, not that I would have known where to look. It wasn't until Marc—the marshal came to the home that I knew you'd dragged him into this life, made him your accomplice while you robbed and killed people."

"If I can't trust my son to guard my back, who can I trust?"

His tone was bitter as he turned away.

Nate straightened from where he'd crouched to build the fire. Abigail planted her feet so she wasn't tempted to cross to it, to warm herself. She wanted nothing Nate or Joseph had. She only wanted her brother safe.

"How did you know where to find me?"

"We ran into the Comanches who were looking for you," Nate said. "We followed you to the fort."

Her entire body still ached from that journey. "And you didn't let yourself be known? We were unarmed and cold."

"We couldn't risk exposing ourselves to him. But when he sent you away..."

She flinched.

"We knew we had to come for you," Abe concluded.

And now what?

* * *

"MARSHAL! MARSHAL!"

Marcus dismounted in the town of Padilla and turned to see a vaguely familiar middle-aged couple hurrying down the board-walk toward him. He frowned and straightened, exhausted from riding hours in the cold and snow. He didn't want to deal with someone's complaint.

How did they know he was a marshal, though? Why were they familiar to him?

"Marshal, your wife!" The woman gripped his arm. "She was taken from the stage by three men. It was horrible."

His...Abigail. The realization penetrated his tired mind, snapping him alert. "What? Abigail? How? Was anyone hurt?"

"No, no one was hurt. The riders came and stopped the stage, called her name. She got out and they took her. She seemed to know them."

"How long ago was this? Which direction did they take her?" He gripped the saddle horn, determined to go after her.

But he couldn't do that to this horse. "Follow me to the stable and tell me what you know. I need to get a fresh horse."

The couple hesitated. Marcus drilled them with a look and they fell in line, following him across the muddy road to the stable. But by the time he traded in his horse—and a few dollars —he was certain Abigail had gone off with Joseph and Abe.

Had she planned that all along? The chill in his gut had nothing to do with the temperature. Was that why she'd come with him?

"Did she seem surprised to see them?" he asked.

The woman's eyes widened. "Why, yes."

"But they didn't force her to accompany them."

"No, she held her hand up to the man, and he pulled her onto the back of the horse. The soldier you sent to protect her fired after them, but they rode off, the four of them on three horses."

"Where's Sergeant Lufkin?" He'd get the information on location and direction from him, and go after them, maybe get the man to accompany him on the search. He'd been paid to look after her, after all.

He had to get to Abigail and make sure she was safe.

* * *

ABIGAIL WOKE up in the one-room cabin at the sound of hushed voices from the table near the fire. She was warm for the first time since she'd left Marcus's arms in the fort. Despite the chinks in the walls, the cabin was close enough to the canyon walls that the wind didn't blow through, though the air was still chilled. The cabin was dark except for the light of the fire, casting the three men at the table in shadow. She wrapped herself in the blanket and rose to join them.

Joseph looked at her sharply then turned back to the conversation with Nate and Abe. Abe nodded at her and pulled out a chair, silently inviting her to join them.

Only then did she focus on what they were discussing—a bank robbery.

"Why are you robbing another bank after robbing the train?" she asked at a lull in the conversation.

Joseph scowled.

"We got separated from the rest of our crew on the train robbery," Nate said. "We didn't get our share."

"We didn't get separated," Joseph said bitterly. "They double-crossed us, putting us in the line of fire and taking off with all the money. So we have to make up the loss another way, and the last robbery was a bust."

Abigail wondered how he'd been surviving the years since her mother's death. Her mother had been the architect of their most successful heists. She didn't think Joseph had the same canny mind.

"We thought we'd use you as a distraction," Nate said. "Like the old days."

Her blood chilled. "You want me to take part in a bank robbery?" How could she? She was in love with a marshal.

"You wouldn't be doing the robbing, just would occupy their attention so we could slip in and do the job," Nate said. "You remember how it's done."

She remembered she'd been young and foolish and in love with him, yes. She'd had nothing to lose. Now she knew, whether Marcus loved her or not, if she was caught with these three men, she would hang.

"We need you, Abigail," Abe said, his dark eyes pleading, reminding her of when he'd been a boy.

"I can't." She drew the blanket tighter around her shoulders, against herself. "I was sent away last time, to the home for wayward girls. This time, I'm not a girl anymore. I can be tried and executed. You can be tried and executed." She leaned forward and touched her brother's arm. "Abe, we can start a new life together, we can get some land, we can ranch."

He pulled his hand out of her reach. "And we need money to do that, to buy the land, to buy the animals and the feed. We need something to start."

"There are ways other than breaking the law." She couldn't let him do this, couldn't let him put himself in danger again.

Joseph pushed to his feet. "This is because of the marshal, isn't it? You spread your legs for him, and now you think like him."

Her face heated at his crass assessment of her relationship. She wanted to tell him yes, this was because of the marshal, because of a future she wanted, a future she hadn't known she wanted. A future she wouldn't have if she was a fugitive from the law.

"I want to live a long and happy life," she countered. "I want that for Abe, too."

"This will be my last job," Abe said. "Then we can get that ranch."

She sat back in the chair, looking into her brother's eyes and not believing him. This wouldn't be his last job. He was too like their mother, too like Joseph. "I can't do it."

Nate gave Joseph a look. The older man returned it for a moment before motioning to his son.

"We need to see to the horses," he told the boy.

Abe looked from Nate to Abigail, hesitant.

"Abe." Joseph's tone sharpened, and her brother jumped to his feet to follow his father.

Abigail eased back toward the fire, wanting distance between herself and Nate. She didn't trust him, not the way he'd sent her family out, not the way he was looking at her. She tried to remember if she'd seen a poker near the fireplace, and she mentally mapped an escape to the door.

When he rose from the table, her heart jumped into her throat. He gave her a smile, one she recognized, and it chilled her more than the air surrounding them.

"You'll do this, or I'll shoot Abe in the back," he said, his tone easy, but with an underlying threat she understood. "No one will know I did it—they'll think he died in the line of fire. But this is the best plan we have, and you will help us, or you'll lose your brother."

He didn't wait for her answer, but turned and strode out the door, leaving her to collapse on the bed and bury her face in her hands.

* * *

MARCUS MOTIONED to Sergeant Lufkin in a silent signal as they approached the mouth of the canyon. They'd reconnoitered from above to get the layout, and now knew just where the cabin lay in relation to their approach.

Marcus hadn't seen smoke rising from the chimney, nor had he seen any horses. Had they missed the crew? Had they gone to another hideout?

The men approached with caution. The snow had stopped hours ago, but drifted against the door of the cabin, proof it hadn't been opened in a while. Marcus dismounted and lightly looped his reins over the fence. He drew his gun and dragged the door open against the snow.

The cabin retained some warmth from an earlier fire, banked now. Marcus lit a lantern to look around, to find proof Abigail had been here.

And then he saw it, there by the wall. The battered satchel. She had been here. His heart jumped. But where was she now?

* * *

"You look really pretty," Nate said, leaning against a table in the mercantile, arms folded over his chest as he inspected Abigail's new clothes, a crisp white shirt and a blue woolen skirt. "I forgot how pretty you are."

And she'd forgotten how charming he could be. So different from Marcus, who didn't try to charm at all, that she had to hide a smile. Nate would interpret her smile to mean something else. Instead, she brushed her hands briskly over the heavy fabric of the skirt, trying not to think about the reason he had brought her here.

"Seems silly to compliment me when you're forcing me to do this."

"It's the best plan we have. We do it right, no one needs to know you were part of it."

"I know I'm part of it."

He pushed away from the table, leaning close. She refused to back away, but her breath caught in her throat. She recognized the viciousness snapping in Nate's eyes. She wanted to run, far and fast, but she couldn't leave Abe with these men, couldn't risk that Nate was as good as his word and would shoot her brother in the back.

"What happened to you? When did you become such a prim and proper miss?"

"I'm...not." She didn't know why his words caused offense. Nothing he said to her should affect her. As soon as this job was over, she was taking her brother and going, and never thinking about Nate again.

"Sure you are. The girl I knew was game for anything."

"Maybe then I didn't know what was at stake. I didn't understand I could die. That the only family I had left could die." She looked over her shoulder, out the window onto the street. She couldn't see Joseph and Abe, but they were out there, making a dreadful mistake.

Nate scowled. "It's being in the company of that marshal, I think, making you think you're better than us. But not so good that you can't warm his bed."

She drew in a sharp breath and stepped back, her hands curling into fists. The girl he was talking about would have slapped his face, not caring that they were in the middle of a mercantile, with people from the town around them.

"Look at that, you're blushing. I didn't think you knew how to blush. Did you show him the things I taught you?"

This time she leaned close. "You taught me," she said through her teeth, "to have low expectations."

His nostrils flared, and for a moment, she thought he would hit her. She braced herself for the blow, but it didn't come. Instead, she looked into the warning gaze of the proprietor.

"Is your business here concluded?" the woman asked sharply.

Nate took a moment before stepping back, his eyes hooded. "Yes, ma'am, we're done."

"Then please be on your way. I don't want trouble in my place."

Abigail saw something flash in Nate's eyes that chilled her to the bone, something mean that promised retribution. Had he always been mean, and she hadn't recognized it because she'd been young and foolish?

She turned to lead the way out of the mercantile, head down. She didn't want the woman to be able to give the lawmen a detailed description of her when this was over. Purchasing supplies in the same town with the bank they planned to rob seemed like a mistake. If the locals placed her with Nate and Joseph, she'd be arrested for sure. The plan smacked of desperation, and she knew Joseph too well when he was desperate. He made mistakes.

"Let's have some lunch," Nate suggested, a little too loudly, taking her arm as he guided her from the store.

In response, her stomach grumbled, but not out of hunger. She hadn't been able to convince Abe to leave with her. He thought they'd do one more job and be set. He didn't remember her mother saying the same thing, time and again. He'd been too young when she died. If he thought robbing this small-town bank was going to set him up for life, he was more naive than she expected.

If only she could get him away from Joseph, even for a little while. She might be able to make him see the futility of this path. But Joseph had made sure they had no time alone together.

Nate made a show of guiding her toward the hotel, with its restaurant, so anyone who overheard them would see they were heading to lunch. But he led her around the corner, past the hotel to the bank. Then he urged her to step inside while he leaned nonchalantly against the wall, lighting a cheroot, the picture of a man waiting for his lady to do business.

Her heart thundered as she stepped into the bank, holding her new reticule in front of her, as if it had anything in it.

"Miss, we're closing for lunch," the man behind the counter told her.

She lifted wide eyes to him. Part of the distraction was that he'd be in a hurry to get rid of her and wouldn't be paying attention to what was going on around him.

"I'll only be a minute. I just need a few dollars for lunch." She stepped up to the counter, ignoring his agitation, and the door behind her burst in.

"Hands in the air," Joseph ordered.

She swung around, her hands raised, more out of reflex than because they'd planned it, to see Joseph and Abe holding guns on the clerk and the manager behind him. Abe was supposed to have been the lookout, and Nate was to have joined Joseph inside. Anger at Nate almost overwhelmed her despair. Seeing Abe holding a gun, his dark eyes bright above the kerchief that covered the lower part of his face, gave her a jolt. He was enjoying this. And he'd likely done it before.

She stepped back when she wanted to rush forward, wanted to warn him, to pull the gun from his hands, to drag him out of here. She was too late. She'd waited too long. He was too like their mother.

The tears that filled her eyes were real as she pressed back against the counter, as Joseph rushed forward, thrusting a bag at the clerk.

"Everything you have."

The gunshot outside made her buck as if she'd been shot. Footsteps vibrated on the boards outside the bank and the doors swung inward. She saw the raised gun barrels of the two men who stormed the bank before Abe did, and she launched herself at her brother as he turned, his own gun raised.

The explosion of a shot deafened her to everything but the sound of her name.

"Abby!"

Marcus. And everything went black.

$\mathcal{M}$arcus paced outside the surgeon's office, his blood threatening to burst out of his skin. He kept his eyes open until they threatened to shrivel up and fall out, because every time he closed them, he saw Abigail fall, saw her blood spread across the pristine white blouse.

At first he'd thought she'd just tripped, had hoped the sheriff's bullet had missed.

But the blood, so much blood. He lifted his hand to see her blood dried in the creases.

Once he'd shackled her brother and tossed him to the wooden floor behind his father, where the sheriff took over, he'd stripped off his jacket and dropped to his knees beside Abigail.

The acrid scent of gunpowder burned his nose. Her eyes had been wide with pain and shock, her mouth opening and closing as she struggled for breath. The wound just below her shoulder pulsed blood. He wadded up his jacket and pressed it to the wound. She hadn't said anything, just reached up and clutched his hand.

Her strength faded quickly and her hand had gone limp in his, scaring the hell out of him. He'd swept her into his arms, shouted for directions to the surgeon and run over here.

The scream lifted the hair on the back of his head, and ended abruptly. That scared him more than the scream. Despite the surgeon's order to stay out here, he slammed through the door.

The surgeon snapped his head up and scowled. Marcus's gaze riveted on the blood coating the man's hands. Abigail's blood.

"She fainted," the surgeon said. "She's not feeling it now."

"Did you get the bullet?"

"Not yet."

"Is it—?"

"Looks like it's wedged against her shoulder blade. Going to have to dig a bit."

Marcus's stomach roiled at the image of the man stretching her pretty skin, already mutilated by the bullet she'd taken, throwing herself in front of her brother.

"There was a lot of blood."

"It didn't hit an artery, but it did come close to her lung. I see a tear there, and some bleeding."

Jesus. "How much longer?"

"Get the hell out of here and let me do my job. Maybe you should go do yours."

Walking out of the room was one of the hardest things he'd ever done. But he kept walking, out the door and down the street to the sheriff's office.

Nate Holland's body was stretched out on a table in the center of the office, a bullet through his black heart. Marcus had acted reflexively when Nate lifted the gun in his direction from his position by the front door of the bank. Probably the same reflex had the sheriff shooting at Abe—and Abigail throwing herself in front of him.

Beyond the office, Joseph and Abe were locked in the cell. Abe jumped to his feet and gripped the bars.

"How is Abigail?"

Marcus glowered at the boy who'd put his sister in danger, at the one she'd die for, but softened a bit when he recognized the real concern in the young man's eyes.

"She's at the surgeon." He crossed to come eye to eye with the boy. "She put her life on the line for you. What the hell was she doing there in the first place?"

"She was part of the plan," Joseph said. "She was the distraction."

His stomach sank. She was an accomplice. If she came through the surgery, she'd have to be arrested and tried.

But that didn't make sense—her whole goal had been to get Abe away from the life of a criminal. Had she found she missed the life? Nate Holland had been her first lover. Had he drawn her back in? He couldn't believe that she would change her mind so soon after reuniting with her outlaw family.

Unless reuniting with them had been her plan all along, returning to the life she'd always known. Had she played on his sympathies to get to her family? Had she lied to him?

The thought made bile rise in his throat. Everything made sense now, how she'd run away from the home to join him, how she'd seduced him, offering sex to lull him. All the while she was planning to break the law.

He stepped away from the bars as anger roiled through him, tightening his fists. He turned to the sheriff. "When will the circuit judge be in town?"

"Beginning of the week. You're in luck." The older man smiled at the outlaws, showing yellowed teeth. "You could be hanging by Wednesday."

The image of Abigail dangling on the end of a rope, the rough fibers biting into her tender skin, turned Marcus's stomach, and he barely made it out the front door before he vomited.

* * *

ABIGAIL'S entire body was on fire, spreading from her shoulder, all through her chest and head. Even her legs were hot.

She dragged her eyes open to find herself in an unfamiliar room with raw board walls, though the boards had no gaps in them. She'd be grateful for a cool breeze right now, anything to cool her heated skin. She attempted to lift her arm to push her hair from her face and pain ricocheted through her. What...?

Blood roared in her ears, but beyond that she heard two men's voices. She forced herself to focus on their words, which sounded like an argument.

"She can't be moved," an unfamiliar voice said.

She held her breath, as if that would stop the pain long enough for her to understand.

"I need to take her."

She didn't know that voice either, and frowned. She'd expected it to be Marcus, but the voice was gruffer. Take her where?

"She's not going anywhere," the first voice assured. "She's safe here."

Safe. She liked that word.

She turned her head—more pain—to look at her chest, felt the pull of her flesh beneath the hurt.

And then she remembered. She twisted, causing yet more pain, to find herself alone in the room. The window was covered with a proper white curtain,, sheer enough to let her know it was still daylight out.

Where was Abe? Was he safe? Had she saved him? The pain in her shoulder was overpowering, so she knew she'd taken the bullet, but had it been enough to save her brother?

She tried to draw in a breath to call for someone to help, but white heat swept through her body, blinding her for a moment. She laid on the bed, gasping for breath as she tried to find peace, or if not peace, a place inside her without this agony.

"Miss Vincent?"

An unfamiliar voice from behind her made her flinch, sending the fire through her body again. When her eyes could focus again, she looked up into faded blue eyes in a creased, bristled face.

"Hurting?"

"My brother?"

"In jail."

She winced. "Hanging?" Each word sliced through her.

"The judge will be here Monday."

Monday. Today was Thursday. She needed to talk to Marcus. "The marshal?"

"He left yesterday afternoon. Haven't seen him since."

She shook her head, which only made her dizzy. "Not possible. He...helped me when I was shot."

"Day before yesterday, Miss Vincent."

"What?" Her mind was hazy, but to have lost two days? So it was Saturday, and the judge would be here day after tomorrow. How could she have even slept through this pain?

The answer came to her when the man lifted a vial to her lips. She recognized the scent of laudanum, something Mrs. McBride had used regularly, and tried to turn her head away. But it touched her lips, poured into her mouth and down her throat. She choked, trying to push the liquid out before it carried her back to oblivion. She'd already lost days to the medication. If the trial was coming, she had to prepare, had to plan. But she couldn't get it out, and it trickled down her throat. A sob shook her body before she drifted off again.

The next time she opened her eyes, a face she did know hovered over her.

The lined face of the man who'd shot her.

"Miss Vincent," the sheriff said in a gruff voice. "You're under arrest."

CHAPTER 9

*W*here was Marcus? Abigail shivered in the jail cell, wrapped in a blanket, colder than she'd been in the falling snow, colder than she'd been as she and Marcus had made their river escape from the Indians. Fever, she knew.

The sheriff had told her there was no point in trying to heal her, since she'd be hanging on Monday anyway.

Hanging. Tears choked her. No one believed Nate had threatened Abe's life if she hadn't cooperated. Nate was dead, and even if he lived, he probably wouldn't have defended her.

If Marcus was here, he would listen. He would believe her. She was sure of it.

"Where's the marshal?" she asked through chattering teeth.

Behind her, in the next cell, Joseph scoffed.

The sheriff didn't look in her direction. "He took off. Had other business to see to."

What other business? she wanted to scream. He hadn't told her of any other cases. Though, honestly, he hadn't told her much, had he? She knew little of his life, of his family, of his home. All she knew was his touch, and his drive.

And that he'd rushed to her side when she was shot.

So where was he now? Did he believe she'd entered the bank of her own free will? She supposed she'd never know. The judge was due to arrive in a few hours, and she'd be dead by the time Marcus got back to town.

The sobs took her by surprise, ripping through the pain in her shoulder, and deeper. She hadn't thought she'd allowed herself the fantasy of a life with Marcus. She shouldn't have such lofty goals as the daughter of an outlaw, in any case. She might have been his mistress, though, in a house of her own where he would come to her and they would make love with abandon, without worrying about others and what they would think.

All of that had been in her head, but clearly not in his. She huddled deeper into her blanket and sniveled.

The hand on her shoulder surprised her, and she turned to look at her brother through bleary eyes. His own eyes were sad, and watery, too. She reached out to take his hand and linked their fingers together as they sat in silence, looking at each other through the bars. At least she'd found him. At least they'd die together.

* * *

ABIGAIL SAT in the stiff chair in the sheriff's office waiting for the judge. The clerks from the bank sat nervously against the wall, avoiding looking at the three of them lined up in chairs, their hands shackled in front of them. Avoiding them was difficult to do in this small room. Abigail choked on pleas for mercy, resisted the urge to throw herself at their feet and beg them to tell the judge she had nothing to do with the robbery.

The sheriff had bought her a new skirt and blouse. Her other blouse had been cut from her, and her skirt was bloodstained. He couldn't have her going to the gallows so bedraggled, she supposed.

She stopped herself from touching her neck, trying to push

the imagined sensation of the rough rope against her tender skin away. She'd stopped crying. She had no tears left. She'd hang, and could only hope she was heavy enough for the rope to snap her neck instantly.

She reached for Abe's hand, the chains of their handcuffs rattling against each other as she did so. He trembled, holding back tears, she knew, afraid to let them fall in front of Joseph. Even with hours to live, he was afraid of the man who'd led him —led them all—to their deaths.

The door opened behind them and Abigail's spine snapped straight. She turned to watch the tallest man she'd ever seen stride into the room behind the sheriff. The two men walked past the three of them before the judge took a seat at the sheriff's desk. He shuffled some papers then looked at them, starting with Joseph, his brown eyes hard, his nostrils flared, his lips in a grim line. The man's gaze slid past Abigail, then back, his eyes widening just a little.

"You are her spitting image," he muttered.

Her mother. Did everyone know her? Did everyone expect Abigail to be like her? Would her resemblance to her mother be her doom?

The judge considered her a long moment, then turned back to the papers in his hands. "The charges are armed robbery of a bank. The three of you, and a fourth, who was a lookout and who is now deceased." He looked at Joseph. "This is not your first crime, and now you've brought your children into it. Was it your plan to watch them hang?"

Joseph said nothing. Abigail chanced a look out of the corner of her eye to see his jaw set, his face expressionless.

The judge turned to Abigail next. "Not your first crime, either. You used to ride with the deceased, Nate Holland. You were his lookout, and were sent to the home for wayward girls to turn you around. I'm sorry to see that didn't work."

She was too frozen by the truth of his words to move.

Finally, he turned to Abe. "This is your first arrest. Not, I think, your first crime, though."

"He was holding a gun on me," one of the clerks blurted from his seat by the wall.

The judge held up a hand without looking at the clerk. "As far as first crimes go, this is serious. I'll hear from the two witnesses before I make my final decision."

Final. As if he'd already made up his mind.

The door behind them swung open again, and this time, Abigail's jolt was hard enough to send pain shooting through her from the hole in her shoulder. Panic almost sent her out of her chair as Marcus strode into the room, his long legs carrying him to the judge's desk in three steps. He didn't spare her a glance, didn't acknowledge her at all, and a different kind of pain rolled through her. Another man was with him, who looked a little worse for wear in following the marshal's path.

The judge sat back in his chair to scowl up at Marcus.

"What is the meaning of this, Marshal? I'm holding court."

"Yes, sir, I know, and I tried to get here sooner, but Mr. Corbett here didn't travel too well. I apologize for my tardiness."

The judge looked past Marcus to the shorter man. "And who is Mr. Corbett?"

"He's the lawyer I hired to represent Miss Vincent and her brother."

The judge's face went slack for a moment. "You hired a lawyer to represent the people you arrested? I believe that's the first time that's been done."

"Maybe so, your honor. But I didn't arrest Miss Vincent and Abe. The sheriff did. If you wouldn't mind, sir, I filled Mr. Corbett in on most of the details, but if we could give him a few minutes with the defendants..."

He'd hired a lawyer. He'd hired a lawyer to save her life. Hope swelled in Abigail, and she tightened her fingers in her skirt, willing him to look at her.

The judge still scowled. "I've already started the proceedings."

"Ten minutes, Judge," Marcus pleaded. "We're talking lives here."

Abigail held her breath until the judge gave a brief nod. The lawyer turned and motioned to her to step into the cell, but she sat frozen, wanting to look into Marcus's eyes, see his reason for helping her. But he didn't look at her, instead walking out the way he came in. Stiffly, she stood and followed Mr. Corbett into the cell, where Abe joined her, sitting on the cot.

"The marshal believed the two of you were coerced into participating in the robbery," Mr. Corbett began.

Hope soared, making Abigail dizzy. Someone would believe her at last. Marcus believed her. But was it enough, with Nate dead and unable to admit what he'd done?

She told Mr. Corbett her side of the story in a rush, clutching Abe's fingers in hers. The man nodded, encouraging her to go on. She wasn't sure if she saw understanding in his eyes, or if she was imagining it, imagining an ending where she'd walk out into the sunlight, a free woman, her brother by her side.

Without a word to her, he turned to Abe. "Now, son. Your story."

Abe hadn't talked much since the arrest, too like his father in that way. "I don't have a story."

"Of course you do, son. How did you end up in this sorry state?"

"My pa and I planned a bank robbery with Nate Holland, and we carried it out."

"No!" The word escaped Abigail on a gasp, the image of her brother swinging just too much to bear. She squeezed his hand. "You were going to be lookout. You didn't know until we got to town that Nate intended to be lookout, and to send you inside. You didn't know."

Abe turned his sad eyes to her. "I'm sorry you got hurt, Abby. I truly am. You shouldn't have been there, that's true. She didn't want to go, and Nate insisted. But I made a choice." He turned back to Mr. Corbett. "I followed my father into the bank."

Desperation wiped away all her earlier hope. "He was forced," she insisted, leaning forward, clasping her hands together so she wouldn't grab onto Mr. Corbett, try to make him see. "Maybe not the same way I was, but as sure as I'm sitting here, he had no choice, not with his father being who he is, expecting what he expected from Abe. Please, Mr. Corbett, you have to make the judge see that."

Why wasn't Marcus here, helping her? She turned her head, but couldn't see him, though she heard the low rumble of his voice.

"Mr. Corbett, I need you to return to the courtroom now," the judge said.

"But—" Abigail protested, gripping Abe's arm.

Mr. Corbett held up a hand to show he was done then extended the same hand, palm up, toward the cell door, inviting her to lead the way back to the makeshift courtroom. Crushed, Abigail forced herself to her feet and walked back into the sheriff's office. She no longer had the strength, the pride, to hold her head up. She'd been offered hope only to feel it strangled from her like her very breath. She didn't seek Marcus's gaze as he sat behind her, barely heard the judge announce that they'd hear from the witnesses.

She listened to the clerks' accounts as if they were speaking about someone else, someone else's life, someone else's actions. An edge of excitement colored their voices, but it couldn't cut through her despair.

The judge heard from Mr. Corbett, who merely reiterated what Abigail had told him, word for word. She was impressed that he had such a good memory, but that wasn't going to save her, wasn't going to save Abe.

The judge cleared his throat when Mr. Corbett was done speaking. "Will the defendants please rise?"

Abigail did, though her legs went watery for a moment before she caught herself on the back of the chair and straightened.

"I find the three of you guilty," the judge declared.

Abigail's vision went dark at the edges, and the little she'd eaten for breakfast rose in her throat. She battled it back, wishing her last meal had been something more than a biscuit and jam. The chill that ran all over her body had nothing to do with the fever or the temperature outside. She was going to die.

"Joseph Two Rivers Running, you led your son into a life of crime, putting that gun in his hands. For that alone, I should hang you, but I will not."

Abigail's head snapped up.

"Marshal Grey has offered to take you to the nearest penitentiary, where you will serve no less than twenty years. He has also offered to take in Abe and Abigail, seeing to their rehabilitation himself. For any other man, I'd not consider it, but I find Marshal Grey to be the most honorable man I've met, and I'm inclined to go along with his offer. I know he will do what is best for the two young people."

Abigail dropped back into her chair, unable to hold herself upright as she struggled to comprehend the judge's words. She wasn't going to die? None of them were?

For the first time since Abe declared his guilt to the lawyer, accepting his death, she found the strength to face Marcus. His gaze was steady, strong, but he didn't touch her, not a reassuring touch, nothing. She was vaguely aware of the judge adjourning court, of the sheriff removing her shackles. For a moment, she felt so light she thought she might float to the ceiling, but she caught herself, unable to bring herself to understand what had happened.

By the time she brought herself back to earth, the judge had walked out, and only the sheriff and Marcus remained with the three of them.

"I don't understand." She had to force the words out, so they were breathy, barely audible. If only he'd touch her, she'd know this was real.

He turned his hat around in his hands. "I'll be escorting Joseph to prison. Then I'll come back for the two of you."

"And then what?"

He glanced at the sheriff, who nodded. Marcus took Abigail's good arm and guided her out the front door of the jail, leaving her family behind. She was aware enough of the gallows beside the sheriff's office, of the people on the boardwalk giving her a berth, looking at her arm in its sling and whispering behind their hands. She was the woman who'd been shot robbing a bank. What little reputation she had was ruined. How could Marcus love her now?

She forced her attention to him.

"I didn't think he'd acquit you, not with the evidence. This was the best deal I could make, to take you and Abe with me."

She placed a hand over her unsettled stomach. She knew he was right—they wouldn't have walked free. "Why?"

He rocked back on his heels, his brow furrowed. "Why?" he repeated.

"Why did you do that?"

He angled his head. "Are you—why are you asking me that?"

She passed her good hand over her hair and pressed it against her temple. "Because. I don't think it's common for a marshal to take responsibility for an outlaw, much less two."

He blew out a breath, glanced around, and took her good hand, drawing her around the side of the building, away from the gallows. This time he didn't release her hand, instead rubbed his thumb in a circle against her palm. When she met his gaze, this time he didn't look away.

"It's not common for a marshal to be in love with an outlaw— or an outlaw's daughter, anyway." With his free hand he touched her cheek, his brows creasing briefly when he contacted her warm skin. "I don't have a home, Abby, you know that, right?"

Perhaps it was the fever, but she didn't follow. "I didn't, but..."

"I need to live in New Mexico, that's my jurisdiction, you understand. We can find a place for the two of us, and Abe, but I'm going to be taking Abe with me, teaching him how to be on the right side of the law. I think that will be good, be what he needs."

She was watching his lips, hearing what he was saying, but not seeing her place in this plan. "He does." She heard the question in her own voice.

"Abby, you're the strongest woman I know. I never knew if I could find a woman strong enough to deal with the issues of my job."

"That's why you want to help me?"

"No! God. No." He took both her hands in his. "When I saw you run in front of your brother, you took years off my life. I thought I'd lost you. I've never seen anyone love someone enough to do something like that. I would like..." He brought her hand to his lips. "I would like to give you a reason to love me that much."

She opened her mouth and closed it when he lowered her hand to her side again.

"Will you marry me, be my wife and show me what that kind of love is?"

Her head was swimming, but she was no longer blaming her fever. "You want to marry me?"

He stepped close and curved his hand around her head, threading his fingers through her hair. "I want to marry you. Say yes."

She hoped the kiss she gave him was answer enough.

EPILOGUE

 *hree months later*

MARCUS DREW up the wagon on the rise above the shiny new clapboard house, with its split rail fence and the bones of a barn to the east. Abe pulled his horse alongside.

"Your new home," Marcus said.

Her only home, built by Marcus and Abe, who'd lived out on the land while she'd stayed in a room in town, waiting, picking out housewares, something she'd never needed before.

Her home, one she'd make with Marcus and Abe, and maybe someday with children. The dreams she hadn't dared to dream had come true.

ABOUT THE AUTHOR

Emma Jay has been writing longer than she'd care to admit, using her endless string of celebrity crushes as inspiration for her heroes. Emma, married 35 years (wed at the age of 8, of course) believes writing romance is like falling in love, over and over again. Creating characters and love stories is an addiction she has no intention of breaking.